MAGICALLY
BLENDED
HUNTED WITCH AGENCY - BOOK 5

Magically Blended

Copyright © 2018 by Rachel Medhurst

ISBN: 978-1719249232

Published in 2018

This book is dedicated to Devon

Other Books in this Series

1

His breath was shallow, uneven. The paleness of his skin made it seem as if he'd passed into the spirit world. And, yet, I could feel his faint heartbeat against my fingers where they rested over his wrist.

"He's lucky he didn't die," Kurt said, hobbling over on his crutches.

It felt like forever since we'd disarmed a bomb outside of an office building in Edinburgh. But, here we were, only five days later. Kurt was healing quickly, his shattered legs setting beautifully back into place.

"You say that to me every day." My sigh was audible.

Shaking his head, Kurt handed me a pestle and mortar. This had been our routine for the last few days. I'd sit, feeling sorry for myself, praying to mother earth that Gerard would wake up. And, Kurt would distract me by forcing me to grind herbs for his healing elixirs.

"I say it because he needs to hear what a fool he is."

"No," I said as I ground the cardamom seeds. "He doesn't need to hear that while he's in a coma. He needs to wake up so we can tell him to his face."

Thumping the pestle down into the stone mortar, I gritted my teeth and pushed as hard as I could. Anything to try and get the anger out. Why had he been so stupid? We were coping with the bomb. He didn't need to help me, it would've been better if he'd let me die.

The energy drained from me as I slumped into the chair. A slight breeze wafted in from the cracked window, bringing the smell of the Thames with it. We had relocated back to the agency building as soon as we could.

"I'm working on an idea to help him regain his magic. You've tried to give him some of yours, the way he did when you were low. But, his body is too weak to accept it." Kurt came and sat next to me.

Handing me a sprig of dried green herbs, he gestured for me to add them to the mortar.

"What idea is that? Also, am I going to blow myself up here?"

Crushing the ingredients together, I eyed my boss suspiciously. He'd tried to help me learn in his herbology lessons, but it was going straight over my head.

"Firstly, you're preparing the spices for tonight's curry, you're not doing a potion. Do you really think I'd let you make an actual herb spell?" His tut was accompanied by a wink.

Placing down the pestle and mortar, I sighed as I leant over Gerard, placing my chin on his arm. I'd been staring at him for days. His eyelashes rested on the sunken bags under his eyes. Kurt didn't know if he could hear us, but he encouraged me to speak to him anyway. So far, I hadn't known what to say.

"Well, I was thinking. If you connect to the ley line, then link in to his aura, you might be able to push the magic into him the way you do the dagger."

My head whipped up, my eyes staring at him. He was a genius. Before, I'd only tried to filter my normal magic into him, but if there was a chance I could almost connect him to the ley line, it was worth a shot.

"Let's do it." Getting to my feet, I tugged on Kurt's arm.

Grabbing my wrist, he squeezed gently to get my attention. "It's risky, Devon. Not just for him, but for you, too. I'm concerned about..."

His sentence trailed off as his face flushed. It wasn't like Mr Blunt to hold back. He must have picked up on my little problem.

Slumping back into my seat, I faced him. "I do have an addiction to the magic. I'll be able to get a better handle on it when the warlock link is taken away in a few days."

Justina had kept in contact with Mary, planning the ritual for the solstice. She'd kept me updated, but my concentration hadn't been the best. As long as I turned up, it would be fine.

"Do you know anything about addictions?" Kurt asked me. "It's not as easy as stopping when you feel like it."

"I know."

"Do you?" His gruff voice was tight.

Taking a deep breath, I swallowed the lump that rose in my throat. Seeing Helena, a woman so crazed by addiction to magic, had put me off. And, yet, whenever I'd had the chance to use mine, I'd done it. Even since Gerard had been in a coma.

4

My sideways glance was met with raised eyebrows. Kurt had become a mentor to me. He was grittier than Justina, able to understand me on a different level.

A cough drew our attention to the door. We were in Gerard's room, almost forgetting that there was a world beyond these walls.

My father stood just beside the wardrobe, his hands folded in front of him. "I'm sorry, I didn't mean to overhear."

Oh crap. My father was the last person I wanted to know about my addiction. It wasn't exactly something I was proud of.

Coming over, he took the seat Kurt vacated. "How's he doing?"

We both glanced at Gerard, who was as still as he had been for days. Kurt had made me leave every time they turned him to make sure he didn't get bedsores. Tears burst into my eyes as I traced one of the number tattoos on his arm.

"Not much better. Kurt has an idea to use the ley line. I think it might work to restore his magic enough to help him wake up."

A wet splash landed on my bare arm from the tear that dropped from my cheek. Blinking, I smiled at my father when he put a hand on my shoulder. His calm nature always gave me comfort.

"I heard what Kurt said about you being addicted. I'm worried about you."

I understood why the others would be concerned. The pull to use magic was getting stronger every day. If I didn't do something drastic soon, like get rid of the warlock link, I would be in trouble. I could end up like Helena. And, that wasn't something I was prepared to risk.

"Dad, I don't know-"

"Do you know how many warlocks get addicted to their magic? When I worked with Isaac Senior, I was his support worker."

"Isaac had an addiction?" My frown was met with an amused smile.

Shaking his head, my father took my hand. "No, I was the coven's support worker. So many of them had addictions. They craved magic so much, they would go to the witches to bargain for a hit of theirs, just to make them feel high."

My heart rate increased. My father had been around addicts? He knew how to help them? That wasn't something I knew about him. Although, that wasn't surprising considering my parents hadn't been in my life since I was ten.

"I... I don't do that." My voice was weak.

Sitting up straight, my father, in his grey jumper and black combat trousers, stared at me. His light brown eyes didn't allow me to look away. The slight stubble on his soft chin made me want to reach up and stroke it, just like I had done when I was a little girl.

"You're in denial." Kurt blurted from where he stood at his makeshift medical table. He held his hands up in apology when my father glared at him.

"That she might be, but that's not how we talk to people who have..." He couldn't say it. I wasn't surprised. His daughter succumbing to the dark magic that ran through her probably wasn't what he'd expected. I hadn't expected it either. I was Devon Jinx. Half witch, half warlock, a bit crazy. But, I'd never been into magic in a negative way. Not like Helena.

"Okay," I said, clearing my throat as I made a decision. "Tell me how to overcome it."

I was speaking to them both but looked at my father. If he had experience with addiction, he would be the best person to help me wean off my magic. The thought of working closely with him made my skin warm slightly. It might not be the best

7

reason, but hopefully, he would be there for me.

"It's a process. It doesn't happen overnight. We won't be able to start implementing anything until you get rid of the warlock link. In the meantime, I'd like you to cut back on your magic use. Not altogether, just slightly."

Swallowing hard, I nodded. I was determined to overcome the thing that was drawing me away from my family. If I didn't rectify it, I would do stupid things. Like keep the warlock link. Yeah, it had gone through my mind a couple of times. Which was exactly why I needed my father's help.

"I do need to do this magic thing for Gerard though. I know it's not going to help my addiction, but-"

"I have to agree," Kurt butt in when my father went to protest. "I know it's going against all protocols, considering, but we need to try it. The longer he's in a coma, the worse it is for him."

A rush of minty air expelled from my father's mouth. "Okay, you do what you need to do. I'll go and inform your mother of what's happening. She's currently watching the CCTV cameras."

8

Poor mum. It was a boring job. However, it had to be done. The streets of London were littered with paranormals. The agency had a duty to the people, and the government, to keep surveillance on our kind.

"I'll come and join her soon," I said, standing up.

Opening his arms to me, my father smiled when I frowned. "Can't I give my daughter a hug? I've watched you battle various creatures, destroy a slave trade, defeat your grandmother. I've not been able to help you. You're too strong. You haven't needed me. However, I've never seen you stop to deal with your own shit. Not properly. And, now, I can finally help."

Giggling, I wrapped my arms around him. "You said a naughty word."

As his scent filtered up my nose, my muscles relaxed. There he was, my father. He'd been distant. I'd been distracted. It was pretty ironic that we would bond over my addiction to magic. Nothing was ever normal in the Jinx household.

"Let's get on with it." Kurt came over, almost shoving us out of the way in the process.

The air rushed around me as my father left. My mother wouldn't be as accepting as he was about my problem. Especially since her mother had been in the same position. Or, similar anyway.

"Okay. This might sound strange, but this spell is a conduit for earth magic. The herbs are healing, attracting. So, I'm hoping that by having you place your fingers over his heart, with this on the tips, you'll be able to send magic from the ley line into him."

"Like an electric shock of magic?" I asked, screwing my nose up when Kurt indicated that I scoop out the gloopy green grassy paste.

The colour instantly reminded me of Gerard's eyes. Tears almost erupted as I realised that I hadn't seen them in five days. Somehow, I regained control and swallowed down my sorrow.

"Put your fingers here, like this." Pulling down the blanket to reveal Gerard's bare chest, Kurt placed the tips of his forefinger and middle finger on my man's pec, just over his heart.

My tongue flicked out to lick my lips as droplets of perspiration suddenly formed above them. It had grown hot all of a sudden. What if it didn't work? What if I couldn't bring him back?

"It's okay," my boss whispered, indicating with his head.

Doing as he directed, I pressed gently, the paste making my fingers slide. Closing my eyes, I connected into mother earth, asking her to give me the purest magic of all. Anything to bring Gerard back to me.

As the tingling shot up my legs, the magic followed. Envisaging the pure white flames that had shown on my blade before I disarmed the bomb, I imagined them going down my arms and into Gerard.

Like warlock magic, witch magic could be manipulated to do what the caster was seeing. Although, only ley line magic could be visible. I didn't open my eyes when Kurt gasped, but I could feel the flames licking down the skin on my arms. They drained out of me and into my man.

"It worked." Kurt's voice was so quiet, I almost didn't hear him.

My body was buzzing. A calm, almost blissful feeling enveloped me as I sighed out a breath. This. This was the freedom I craved when I performed magic. It was also why I was addicted.

Opening my eyes, I expected to see bright green irises. Instead, Gerard's pale lids were still closed.

"What do you mean it worked?" I snapped. "He's still in a coma!"

Steadying the shake of my hands by gripping them, I turned to my boss, ignoring the squelch of paste on my fingers.

"I saw the white light go into him. It might take some time for his aura to absorb it. It might be a little while-"

The sound of pounding footsteps caused Kurt to pause. Justina thundered into the room, her cheeks bright pink, her hair escaping from her little ponytail. Her breath was short as she looked at us.

"We've got a problem," she said. "Mackenzie has escaped prison."

2

"This is his last known address," Justina whispered as she checked her tablet.

The thing beeped quietly as she tucked it away. It was often attached to her hand. She recorded every single detail in the high tech gadget. I wouldn't know how to use it, even if they gave me a degree in it. My technophobe mind was resigned to the fact.

"So, Cameron's sister... what is her bloody name?"

Prepping her gun, Justina tucked it into the belt under her jacket. Her long legs were encased in leathers, her boots finishing the hot kickass look. My outfit left a lot to be desired. Jeans with holes so big in them that my legs were more bare than covered and as usual, my trade mark mop of dark hair. Unbrushed.

"Candy Fieldman." Gesturing for me to follow, she checked the street as she stepped out from behind Mackenzie's neighbour's garage.

Justina had revoked the ban on flashing between cities. It would've taken far too long to travel from London to Scotland by train. Fuck what the human government said. We had to find Mackenzie before he put people in danger again.

"Keep your head. No magic, or if you have to use it, only a little, please." Ah, it seemed my other boss had noticed my problem too.

Well, my father had made me promise that I would cut back. Maybe that wouldn't be a bad thing. Especially after I'd accidentally killed five witches in the drug factory.

"What a terrible name," I said, almost as an afterthought.

Approaching the house in the leafy suburb, we kept our footsteps light, casual. The detached house was lit up by the setting sun. It was a warm evening, too warm. I was already sweating.

"I doubt they're here, but it's worth checking." Justina indicated that I went around the back.

Slipping my hand into my pocket, I pulled out my dagger. I wasn't prepared to go into a warlock's den without some sort of protection. I'd tried to fight Mackenzie with my fists, but it hadn't worked very well. Maybe the threat of my blade would ward any enemy off.

It was quiet around the back of the house. The garden was pretty, flowers blossoming in their little beds. Would I ever live on the outskirts of London with Gerard? Would we have little kids running around with our ten dogs and fifteen cats? What? I liked animals.

Double glass doors were on the far end of the house. I couldn't walk in front of the windows, in case anyone was inside. My phone vibrated against my leg just as I ducked under the kitchen window. The sound made me jump, making me almost curse out loud.

The text on my phone was from Justina. Alerting me to sounds in a room on the first floor of the house. Ah, who could it be?

Glancing in the kitchen window, I smiled. No one there. Trying the back door, I twitched when it wouldn't budge. Magic was the only way I could get in. Using it was my lifestyle. How the hell would I beat an addiction to it?

Whispering the spell, I pushed the thought away and silently opened the door. The smell of a home well lived in made me pause. Mackenzie had a life. He was in love. And, that was the problem. He had let himself become obsessed with the idea that he couldn't be in a relationship with his witch.

My gaze traced through to the hallway as Justina crept through a gap in the front door. Either she'd done a spell, or the couple had been careless.

Voices raised above us suddenly. Almost marching down the hallway, I met my boss at the bottom of the stairs.

"You!" Mackenzie shouted from the top.

Shaking his head, he bit his lip. His long leather coat hung from his slumped shoulders. His cheeks grew dark red as he stared at us.

A pretty tall girl came to stand next to the warlock, tugging on his arm. "Let's go," she said, tears streaming down her face. "Please."

Glancing at her, he scowled. "You never fight for me."

His attention returned to us as he dismissed Candy and moved onto the next step. "How did you get here so quickly?"

Justina raised her gun, her feet apart, her stance ready to shoot. I kept my dagger pointing down by my side.

"You don't have to do this, Mackenzie," I said, trying to reason with him.

The slight raise of his eyebrows told me how ironic my words were. What choice did he have? Managing to break out of the agency's prison meant that he had major backup. Surely, Candy Fieldman wasn't strong enough to get past all of our wards?

Looking at the witch, I decided to change tactic. She obviously loved Mackenzie. Why else would she be risking so much?

"Are you seriously okay with him killing people by spiking the drugs your brother deals?"

Justina was obviously proud of my diplomatic approach. Her silence meant that she trusted me to lead with the questions. Candy was a pretty girl. Her long dark hair was messy where she'd obviously been rushing around with her man. Their shared look was fleeting, but the threat in her eyes gave me pause. Was she the one running the show?

"You'll never understand," she said. "Let's go, Mac." Taking his hand, she tried to yank him towards her.

My chest squeezed tightly at the use of my old nickname for Gerard. All the anger that had boiled within me when we had argued about my link to the ley line had disappeared. I just wanted my man back.

"You are determined to kill people," Justina interrupted before they could disappear. "If you continue to run, the government will issue a warrant for your death. They will not tolerate supernaturals who are willing to kill."

The flash of guilt that made Mackenzie cringe was caught by my keen eye. He wasn't in control. That changed everything. Well, kind of. The bastard had still thrown a bomb at me. He would pay for that. Shame it wouldn't be me who was dishing up the punishment.

"If you don't leave now," Candy said. "You'll blow up with this building."

A sudden humming of energy intensified. The pair disappeared just as we made a run for the stairs. Grabbing Justina back, I stopped her from ascending. If the energy in the house was anything to go by, Candy was telling the truth.

"We need to get out of here," I said, dragging Justina to the front door.

She tried to pull back, her initial instinct to search the house for evidence. However, I could feel the magical pulse of the house getting stronger by the second.

Thrusting through the front door, I grabbed my head as a high pitched sound blasted through my ears. Justina caught me before I fell to the ground, my legs giving out from under me. She obviously felt my urgency because she half dragged, half ran me away from the building. We had just reached the footpath when a blast echoed behind us, sending us sprawling into the road.

Smoke choked me as debris littered the ground around us. Justina coughed before she stumbled up to her feet. Sitting up, I cringed as I rubbed my knees where I had scraped them on the concrete. The grazes stung badly, my ripped jeans useless for protection. Maybe my wardrobe was in need of a kickass update.

Staring at the impressive destruction that used to be Mackenzie's home, I shook my head in disbelief. The houses on each side were completely intact. Candy had obviously created a spell to protect them. If they were killing people just to drag Cameron down, why would she care about Mackenzie's neighbours? Something was off.

"Who are you calling?" I asked as Justina dialled someone on her phone.

"The police. Can you do a spell to make it look like the house is intact please? Quickly."

My skin itched all over as I thought about the intensity of the spell she was asking me to cast. It was my job to use magic in the field, but I had promised to rein it in to help deal with my addiction.

Placing my hand on the ground, I took a tiny amount of pure power from the earth beneath me. Whispering an illusion, I covered the torn apart building with the spell. To others, it would look like Mackenzie's house was normal. And yet, as my fingers shook slightly, I stared at the smoking ruins of brick and mortar. We could have been blown up. How many times would the illegal couple risk our lives?

"The police are coming to deal with the destruction." Justina held out her hand to me. "We need to search what's left of the premises before they get here. Just in case any evidence has survived."

Letting her pull me up, I brushed myself down as much as I could. Bits of unknown material clung to my hair as I tried to pry it out with my fingers.

Glancing over her shoulder, my boss gestured for me to follow. Tempering the urge to use magic to filter through the shit left over, I went with her. Physical labour wasn't a part of my job description. Especially when there were a bunch of policemen on their way.

"She had something to hide," Justina said as we picked our way through the shattered hallway and into the small office by the front door.

Going to the desk, I rooted through the drawers. "I think she's controlling him. It seems strange that she's so determined to keep him out of prison. It's a shame they got away."

Stretching up, Justina reached to a shelf that still clung to a partial wall. It was ridiculously dangerous in the building, but I understood why we needed to try and gather any clues before the police descended. If I broke so much of a fingernail while pissing around in MacKenzie's home, I would kill him in more ways than one.

"There's nothing in this desk," I muttered, my gaze drawn to the length of Justina's back as she struggled to reach something.

"I would offer to help, but as I'm probably the length of your legs, I doubt I can offer you anything of value."

Justina's snort was swallowed by the bang of something hitting the ground as she swung her arm. A wooden box smashed open as it landed, spilling the contents onto the light blue carpet.

Bending down, I picked up the vials of clear liquid as a grin spread across my face.

Justina's phone started to ring. Our gaze locked as I held up the evidence that suggested MacKenzie had been in on the poisoning.

"Hello," Justina answered.

The instant tensing of her back made me watch her closely. Chewing on her lip, she listened intently to whoever was on the end of the line.

"Really?" Justina glanced at me, her light blue eyes narrowing on my hand. "That's interesting."

Thanking the person who had obviously given her information, she hung up. Holding out her hand, she indicated that I should give her the drugs.

"These must be the poison," I said, frowning when she shook her head.

Tingles spread up my arms as I gave her the vials and stepped back. The confusion written across her face made my stomach clench in anticipation. Someone had just given her some juicy news.

"That was the lab. The drugs from the factory were clean. There was no trace of the poison that's killing clubbers. It looks like Keith is cleaner than we thought."

Crap. That meant Mackenzie must have a different premises. It seemed that the case wasn't as closed as I had originally thought.

3

Sweat lined my forehead as I came out of the gym. Working out was the only way I could stem the temptation to use my magic. Not only that, it helped to stop the urge to break down and cry every time I thought about Gerard.

The hallway in the agency building led me to the swimming pool. The swimming pool was in the basement. I often escaped work by doing a few lengths. Although the building was only small, there were several floors. A handful of agents lived with Justina and Kurt, but they were rarely around during the day.

Without thinking, I went through the motion of changing into my swimsuit, my mind swirling my thoughts. Keith was still guilty of running part of the drug trade, but his place in Scotland wasn't being used to contaminate the drugs. Why had Mackenzie been in that building the day I had caused an earthquake if he wasn't poisoning the drugs?

Diving into the water, I swum the length of the pool, allowing the cool liquid to ease my tense muscles.

Coming up to the surface, I gasped in a breath, almost jumping out of my skin when Lilia's feet appeared right in front of my face.

"Devon," she said before I could turn to go back the other way.

The witch had become a vital part of the agency. Her vulnerability had warmed me to her when I had rescued her. That sweetness still remained, but her strength had returned. She was now an official agent. Although she never worked in the field, she had slowly become one of my good friends. Especially now that she looked after Kingsley so well when I wasn't around.

"Everything okay?" I asked, brushing my wet hair back from my face.

Grabbing the hem of her dress, Lilia bent down towards me. Her wavy blonde hair was unruly as she reached forward and cupped my chin. "Gerard's awake."

Ripping away from her, I almost drowned. Well, not quite. My head went underwater as I kicked to try and get up again. My shock had caused me to sink.

"Come on," Lilia called as she flip-flopped towards the door.

Placing my hands on the edge of the pool, I hauled myself out. Water ran off me as I almost skipped to catch up. Flinging my towel around me, I didn't bother to wait. Whispering a relocation spell, I paused when I landed outside Gerard's room. Gerard was awake? Gerard was awake.

My heart couldn't make up its mind. One minute it was beating fast, the next it almost stopped. When I had last spoken to him, we hadn't been in a good place. He had then given up all his magic for me. Would he regret it?

Not caring that I was dripping water all over the floor, I entered the room, my gaze instantly seeking my man. He was sitting up in bed, sipping water through a straw. The colour had returned to his cheeks as Kurt fussed over him. My whole body started to shake as I drew nearer.

"Thank goodness you're back," Kurt said, neither of them noticing that I was there. "I don't know what I would do without you, man."

My feet paused. I had never heard Kurt be so open with his male colleague. Tears popped into my eyes as I realised how close we had all become.

"You can come over now," Kurt said, turning to look at me. "Your magic healed him."

His eyebrows rose as I tucked the towel around me. My wet hair stuck to my neck as I avoided Gerard's gaze. Why the hell had I come to see him half naked? Now was not the time to be watering the floor.

Chewing my lip, I moved closer as Kurt left us to it. Finally allowing myself to look into his green eyes, I swallowed the lump that rose to my throat.

My partner, Mr Handsome-man, was resting his head against two pure white pillows. He still needed support. I still needed him. And yet, I couldn't find the words to break the silence.

"Kurt told me that you were able to disarm the bomb."

No. I wouldn't allow him to be the agent with me. He had to know that I was sorry for storming out on him.

Sitting on the bed, I grabbed his hand. "I almost lost you."

His gaze dropped to stare at our entwined fingers. Gently squeezing me, he licked his lips. "I thought I would lose you. You risked your life when you took all that magic into you. You were prepared to die to save all the people that were trapped. You were prepared to die for me."

A shaky breath left me as I nodded. "I told you. I'll do anything to be with you. Anything."

If Gerard chose that moment to tell me that he wasn't going to be with me, I wouldn't be responsible for my actions. He had almost died helping me. There was no way he could pretend that he didn't love me.

"It's not about me anymore," he said, stroking my arm as he let me go. "Your problem with magic is not helping our situation. You say that you could give up both links to witch and warlock magic, but I'm not sure that you really mean it."

"If you're talking about my addiction, I'm going to work on it. My father has offered to help me. The solstice is so close. Once the warlock link has gone, I'll basically be in rehab." The distasteful expression that must have crossed my face made Gerard chuckle.

28

It was good to see him looking so well. It was amazing to smile with him again. My light mood crashed as my body finally relaxed. Gerard wasn't dead. A sob escaped me before I could snatch it back. Moving quicker than I could, Gerard wrapped his arms around me, holding me tight against his chest.

"I love you," I whispered as tears mixed with the water from my hair, smearing across his hunky man chest. "I'm so glad you're alive."

"I should bloody well hope so." His voice was tight.

Pulling away, I looked into his eyes. They were clear, full of clarity. The tinge of colour in his cheeks was the only sign that he was feeling any emotion.

"Devon Jinx," he breathed. "You're crazy."

And, that wasn't what I was expecting to hear from him. Amazing, yes, without a doubt. Kickass, well, I tried. That he loved me more than his gun. Of course. But, no, he stated the obvious.

"Is that-?"

"I haven't finished." His gaze softened as he glanced down the length of me.

My towel was half hanging off, revealing my red swimsuit. I had left a massive patch of wet bed beneath me, although I was starting to dry off.

"I told you before, you're my crazy. Before you decide to get unlinked from the ley line, do one thing for me?"

One thing. I could do one thing. Couldn't I? It would depend on what it was, of course. If he wanted me to meet other men, I would put him back into a coma. Or, maybe he would want me to-

"When the warlock link has gone, spend one week without using any magic so you can remember what it felt like before you gained all your power. If you can cope without it, I'll support your wish to disconnect from both links."

"Does that mean you'll marry me?" Where had that question come from? It was supposed to be the man who asked the woman. Or was it? I suppose not, but still... *not the right time, Devon.*

Threading his fingers into the back of my wet hair, Gerard brought my head nearer to him. His gaze was locked on mine, his breath hitched in his throat. "If you keep running away when conversations get hard, I'm not sure we'll ever make it to a wedding day."

The corner of his lips twitched in an attempt not to smile. My fake glare made Mr

Not Funny pull me closer. As we kissed, a knock on the door went ignored.

It sounded again louder, causing us to pull apart. Groaning, I stroked Gerard's hair. "I know you're worried about my addiction. I am too. I promise that I'm going to deal with it. I'm going to deal with everything so I can be free to live my life."

His sigh was drowned out as the knocking got more urgent. "Sorry to interrupt, but Gerard needs his rest. Now is not the time to have makeup-"

"Come in!" I shouted before Kurt could finish his sentence.

The whole of the agency building would've been able to hear him. As if we needed the other agents to assume that I'd jumped on a man who had just come out of a coma. It might have crossed my mind, but I wasn't that shallow.

The door opened. Both Kurt and Justina came into the room. I kissed Gerard quickly before getting to my feet. Justina's frown confused me until she looked down at my towel.

"Oh, I was swimming when Lilia told me that Gerard was awake."

A slight nod of her head was the only acknowledgement she gave me. "Gerard," she gushed suddenly, going over to him. "I'm so pleased you're awake. You had us worried for a moment."

Ignoring me, she stood beside his bed, her foot tapping the floor. Glancing at Kurt, I held in the mirth that wanted to escape.

"Just bloody hug him or something, woman," Kurt said, coming over with another one of his herb concoctions. "You're making it weird."

Gerard opened his arms, inviting Justina to go closer. She thrust forward, awkwardly throwing her arms around him. Patting him twice on the shoulder, she hurriedly withdrew, her boss demeanour back in place. It took a lot for her to really soften. I felt honoured that she was obviously more comfortable with me. I wasn't surprised, Gerard wasn't exactly Mr Warm to anyone but me.

Kurt put his arm around Justina's shoulder. "Very nice, darling. Why don't you get on with what you really came here for?"

Three of us laughed as Justina swept Kurt's arm off her. Ah, so that's why she'd been so stiff. She trusted Kurt when he said that Gerard was well. Which meant, she was only being polite to her top agent. What was it she actually wanted?

"Fine." She almost snapped, her head turning to me. "Devon, Mary just called. She's ready to prepare you for the solstice. We need to go. Now."

4

"It's weird not having Gerard and Kurt here with us."

Nodding her agreement, Justina marched across the car park after shutting the van door. Once we'd arrived at Mary's, the seer had insisted that we drive to Clava Cairns. She had told us in no uncertain terms that she would not be transported by magic. Apparently, it made her sick.

Shuffling along behind us, Mary grunted. Turning back, I took her bag from her, not giving her a chance to refuse. She had tried to make me leave her alone as soon as she stepped out of the van. However, her huffing and puffing was not getting us into the clearing any quicker.

Her grey hair was loose down her back, her hips waddling as her dress swayed. The long lilac patchwork material was threadbare, but somehow it suited the Celtic seer.

"Go through that gate there," Mary called to Justina.

My boss had stopped by the entrance to Clava Cairns. She was checking something on her phone. Hopefully she would be able to put the case to one side while we got on with whatever it was Mary needed us to do.

"You're both so interested in modern day technology, you've failed to notice the standing stones right in front of you." Mary tutted as she gestured for us to follow her into the clearing.

The grass was springy under my feet as I got closer. There were several tall standing stones placed in a circle around a circular rocky burial chamber. It was ancient. There was no roof, and the stones were only halfway up. However, there was a little entrance into a small area in the middle.

"There are three Cairns here," Mary said as we walked up to one of them. "They are all placed directly in line with the sun. They are pagan, of course. Witches used the alignment of the sun and moon to cast their spells and bury their dead. The tall standing stones that are surrounding the Cairns all play their own part."

Going up to the tallest stone in the clearing, I placed my hand on it. The energy of history was strong, the vibration tickling my fingers.

"That stone was used as inspiration for the television show that has that hunky Scottish man in it." Mary placed her hand on the other side. "You know the one, don't you?"

"Seriously? Jamie Fraser is one of my favourite characters."

"You read?" Justina said, laughing when I growled in her direction.

Her relaxed expression made me smile. She had been on edge ever since Mackenzie had escaped from prison. No one had ever been able to escape. The government were on her back to find him. To say that they were going to make an example of him was an understatement. I hated to think what they had planned.

"These stones hold incredible power on the solstice. They link into mother earth and the moon at the same time." Mary threaded her arm through mine and walked me towards the other end of the clearing.

"It's so peaceful here." My muscles started to relax.

There was something soothing about the presence of so much earth energy. The amount of witches throughout the ages who had probably used these stones made my heart warm.

"Yes," Mary said, her shoulders lowering. "Ever since that show came out, the stones have attracted a lot of attention."

"I can imagine that doesn't help with the natural magic here," Justina piped up from behind.

Slowing down, we waited for her to join us. She had seemed disinterested in helping me with the link. However, I knew that wasn't really the case. She was probably way too focused on the drug case to be worried about me. I always had to go and make things more complicated. Not that I had planned on inheriting the warlock link.

"I'm sorry about this," I said, taking her hands in mine. "I know you don't need it on top of everything."

Confusion crossed her face before she smiled gently. Taking a huge breath, she released it before she looked me in the eye. "I know I've been distracted recently. It's not because of the case. It's something else."

Sharing a look with Mary, Justina raised her eyebrows. The seer nodded as a sharp laugh came from her thin lips.

Okay, this was just getting weird. If Justina wasn't distracted because of Mackenzie Dickhead... Oh, that could work. In fact, that was my new mission. I would come up with as many nasty nicknames for Mackenzie as I could. Anyway, Justina...

Snapping back to attention when Justina's face lit up, I tried not to frown. "What's going on?"

My boss's throat moved as she swallowed hard. Looking at the ground, she mumbled something that I couldn't hear. Tugging her hands, I almost shouted. "What? I can't hear you. You're being strange. It's not like you to be strange."

"I'm pregnant, Devon."

As her cheeks glowed pink, my jaw almost hit the floor. Excitement suddenly bubbled causing me to hop up and down while holding onto my best friend. That's what she had become. Not only my boss, but a best friend.

"I can't believe it!"

Suddenly throwing off her usual calm facade, Justina squealed as she hugged me to her. My face planted into her boobs as she squeezed me tightly. Almost unable to breathe, I choked out a laugh as Mary cleared her throat.

"I hate to put a downer on things, but-"

"Congratulations," a deep male voice interrupted our girly explosion of excitement.

Instantly falling apart, we turned in unison, our exuberance evaporating as we spotted the barrel of a gun. A man, probably in his forties, his hair long and tied back, aimed it directly at us.

"Who are you?" I demanded.

My hand rested on my dagger where it poked out of my jacket. I had a lot of magic, and yet, I knew that I had to keep control. Clava Cairns did not need my magic to ruin it. The purity of the place had to be kept intact.

The man was short, barely taller than me. That was a miracle. I was almost tempted to share my height woes with him. It must be a nightmare for a man to be a short arse. Although, if he went around holding pretty women at gunpoint, he would never make it in life anyway.

"You don't need to know who I am," he said, staring straight at Mary. "But, you can call me Bradley."

Huh? I wasn't exactly the sharpest knife in the weapon cabinet, but had he just completely contradicted himself?

Justina put her hands on her hips. "Look, I'm not in the mood for this. Please state what it is you want."

The queen of diplomacy may well be a thing of the past. Being pregnant, Justina would have hormones rushing throughout her body. Maybe that meant she would let us fight more. A sliver of adrenaline pulsed through me as I imagined cradling her baby in my arms. How would she be able to keep doing her job if she was going to be a mother?

"It's simple," Bradley muttered, coming closer.

Standing in front of Justina, I grabbed my dagger out and held it in his direction. He smirked, his gaze tracing the weapon in my hand. If he dared to underestimate what it could do, I was tempted to show him just for the sake of it.

"He's a seer," Mary said, moving in front of me. "What do you want?"

Wait. I had moved to protect my pregnant lady boss. Why had Mary, an ancient woman, put herself in front of me? Didn't she see that I had an amazing dagger in my hand? What was she playing at?

"I want her." Bradley's eyebrows screwed up.

Had the man just confused himself? It looked like he had no idea what he'd just said. Anyway, if he wanted me, he would have to try and catch me. Not that I wanted to play chase right now.

"Wait," Bradley said, lowering his gun ever so slightly. "No. I want what she has. The link."

Oh boy. If the male seer wanted the warlock magic, every supernatural being would be after me soon enough. Although, was it even possible for them to access any of the power? Why were people so stupid?

"I'd love to help you with that," I said, pushing Mary behind me. "But, you see, I'm not going to. Now, if you'll excuse us, we have something to do."

His laugh made me pause as I went to turn away. Why? Just why?

"You think that I'm powerless," he said, his arm lifting again. "I'm not."

Clearing her throat, Justina drew his attention. Her hands were on her slim hips, her hair tucked behind her ears. "You have exactly one minute to get out of here before I arrest you. The government is getting sick of paranormal creatures fighting. This link will go back to the warlocks and everyone will be happy about it. Do you understand?"

"I've tampered with the stones. There's nothing you can do to disconnect the half breed from them without me. Good luck with that."

Spinning, the seer started to run. My feet were moving before anyone could say a word. Jeez, he was fast. How was he so fast on such short legs?

"Get back here, you little runt," I shouted, my blood boiling at his interference.

He was an insignificant little fool. If a seer was the one who was going to stop me from getting rid of the warlock magic, I would kill him. No guilt, no shame.

My breath huffed in and out as I chased him to the entrance. My willpower held strong as I fought the urge to use my magic to trip him over. If he had tampered with the stones, I wanted to rip his heart out. Okay, maybe my addiction was blurring the lines of professionalism.

"Stop!"

My shout went ignored as he opened the gate and thrust through. My feet skidded to a halt, my boots kicking up grass as the little man disappeared. He literally pushed out of existence. Shit. How had he vanished? He wasn't able to cast spells. In fact, it was rare to have a male seer.

"He's gone," I called to the others as I rejoined them.

Mary was touching the main standing stone, feeling the energy around it. Justina was doing something with her tablet, holding it in the air and moving it around. I knew that she loved to use her technology, but waving it around wasn't going to do much.

"We need to get out of here," she said suddenly, looking at me. "Don't look at me like that, I was checking the resonance of magic around the borders of the clearing. It looks pretty clear except for one space in the car park. Just a slice of energy that doesn't belong here."

"Ah," Mary said, taking my arm and tugging me. "We do need to get out of here then. Bradley must be working with someone who's able to open a slit in time. He probably transported through it."

Wow. I had no idea that was even possible. Why did I not know that? If someone could manipulate a portal, it wouldn't be good for us. Enemies like Bradley would be dangerous if they could access magic. A seer should never be able to get close to it, let alone open a slit in time.

"What is it with paranormals ganging up to work with each other? First Maxwell has a witch prepared to put herself on the line, and now someone is helping Bradley to threaten us. This shit has to end."

Justina tucked her tablet away again, her frown evident as she tried to hide it. "I'm sorry, Mary. It looks like this place has been compromised. I've picked up the data needed to do an analysis. I once showed Devon how to check the DNA of magic. We'll be doing that before we come back. Next time, we'll bring a team with us. We need to keep everyone safe."

Sighing, Mary flicked her hair behind her shoulder as she stroked the stone in front of her.

"I'm afraid," she said, her gaze fixed on the cold hard surface. "Magic is becoming unpredictable. We need you in the world now." Turning to look at us, she clenched her hands into fists. "If you can get control of the underworld, we'll be safe. If not..."

Shivers went up my spine as her sentence was left unspoken. Her energy was heavy, a testament to what she might have seen. Her prophecies tended to come true, which meant only one thing. We had to find a way to work together with other supernaturals to bring down those that wanted to destroy magic.

5

"Devon," my mother said as she walked into the agency library. "We need to talk about these Essex witch vows. Once you're disconnected from the warlock link, we have to do our duty to our ancestors. Otherwise, that MI5 agent won't leave you alone."

Looking up from where I was staring over Justina's shoulder, I nodded quickly. Now was not the time to tell her that I wasn't going to take my vows. The lines around her mouth relaxed as my father came in behind her. He put an arm around her shoulders and squeezed. "See, I told you that Devon would do the right thing when she was able."

Apparently, my parents had been talking about me behind my back. Why didn't that surprise me? Although, it was actually quite nice to have someone to worry about me.

"Paranormal MI5 can wait a few more weeks," Justina said, holding up her tablet. "We'll figure out how to get Devon disconnected without interference from anyone else. I need her to be available to carry on working this case. We need to find Mackenzie and Candy."

My father was watching me, his eyebrows raised. The question in his expression was obvious. How was I doing with the magic? The truth was, I actually didn't feel the urge to use it as much anymore. Just admitting that I had a problem made it less intense for me. How did that work?

"Devon and I have just got back from the lab. The magic that allowed Bradley to disappear isn't in our database. In fact, it's an unusual magic. Its DNA isn't recognised at all. Meaning that there might be a new magic to contend with." Justina tucked her hair behind her ear as my father joined us by the desk.

The door opened as I was about to speak. Gerard strode in, his spine straight and his head held high. His tattoos moved as he reached up to scratch the stubble on his chin. My stomach flipped as his gaze met mine. A small smile tugged at his lips as he stood there. A squeak from Kingsley, who happened to be sitting on his shoulder, made me laugh.

"What's he doing here?" Moving over to them, I stroked my rat as he refused to leave the comfortable rest that was Gerard. "Traitor."

I didn't blame him. If I could lay on Gerard right now, I would. However, not only were things difficult between us, my parents were in the room.

"It's good to see you up and about," my father said, coming over and shaking Gerard's hand. "Devon's been a nightmare since the bomb incident."

Erm. Had my father seriously just embarrassed me? My cheeks warmed as Gerard placed his hand on my father's shoulder and squeezed. "I'm not surprised. I didn't mean to scare you all, I'm sorry."

That wasn't the reply I had expected. In fact, Gerard wasn't exactly his cheery self. Had the coma knocked him back to his old broody self? Well, Mr Gerard Grumpy Bum wouldn't be allowed to stay for long. Not if I had anything to do with it.

Justina cleared her throat to get our attention. "I was just telling the others that we were unable to trace the magic that helped Bradley. I'm also unable to find a match to his name and face."

The door burst open, the wood almost smacking into the wall behind it. The singing voice of Kurt reached us before his body emerged into the room. A smile was plastered across his face. It had been 24 hours since Justina had broken the news of her pregnancy to the team. A rush of warmth started in my heart and spread like tentacles throughout my body. Seeing a man so happy after learning about his child made me all fuzzy inside. Even Gerard cracked a smile when Kurt slapped his back and finished his song.

"Well, good morning, my beautiful souls. And, of course, my beautiful soulmate." Opening his hand, Kurt showed us a pile of small seeds that sat on his palm.

Bringing his other hand out from behind his back, he waved it above the seeds as he whispered a spell. A glow of white ethereal light sunk into the seeds, causing them to burst open and sprout. Within moments stems had formed and grown into a beautiful bouquet of lilies.

"Why have you never done that for me?" My mother asked my father.

They shared an intimate gaze, their love for each other more obvious than I had ever seen. They were quite low-key when it came to public affection.

"Because I'm a warlock, darling," my father said, tapping the end of her nose with his finger. "I can rustle you up a breakfast much easier. These hands are-"

"Okay," I interrupted. "That's enough affection for one day. Shall we get on with it?"

I wasn't about to stand around and watch two older couples be all smoochy to each other when I couldn't even get Gerard to look at me. Well, it might be the other way round. I was struggling to look at him when the others were showing such clear intimacy.

"I suppose it is a little weird having us all paired off." Kurt went over to Justina and handed her the bunch of flowers.

Pretending not to like the gesture, Justina placed the bouquet on the desk. Picking up her tablet, she stared at it before looking up at her man and grinning. Ugh. I needed a sick bucket. There was cute, and then there was not.

Reaching up to stroke Kingsley, I accidentally on purpose let my finger trace Gerard's jaw. It clenched as he glanced at me, his eyes suddenly sparking into life. Was my touch a good thing? Or, was it just the love in the room that made him suddenly relax?

"Right." Justina stood from her seat. "Let me give you all a proper run down."

Everyone in the room went still, their gaze locked onto our boss. When Justina went into agent mode, she demanded attention. Her brains were the backbone of the agency.

"We have two threads to follow right now. It's a priority to get Devon unlinked from the warlock magic on the solstice. At the same time, we need to find Mackenzie and Candy so that we can end this case. I've had an order from the government to issue them both with a death warrant."

Gasps resounded in the room as we all looked at each other. We knew that the government were cracking down on supernatural criminals, but it was the first time that a death warrant had been issued since I had become a part of the agency.

"We only have a few days to prepare for the solstice. I'm thinking about splitting us into teams so that we all have something to focus on instead of having our attention pulled in different directions."

I was about to protest when Justina's tablet started playing the Skype ringing sound. She glanced at it before looking at us. "It's Mary. I'd better answer it."

She pressed something and then turned the tablet to show us Mary's face. The seer grinned and waved, her lined face relaxed as she looked at each one of us. "Hello there," she greeted, her accent seemingly thicker. "I've missed having you all here."

"We only saw you yesterday." I went closer to Justina so I could see Mary clearer.

"Oh, is that you, Gerard, dear?" Mary's cheeks glowed red as she blew a kiss to my man. "It's good to see you up and about. When Justina showed me you through Skype when you were in a coma, I was worried."

A snort exploded from my nose as Gerard's expression blossomed into horror. Justina shook her head vehemently. "I didn't do that."

Mary frowned, her gaze looking off into the distance. "Maybe I just saw it in a dream. I sometimes get confused with reality and my prophecies. You understand."

The lines on Gerard's forehead relaxed as he glanced at me. My laughter was only just under control. The tittering that escaped was the only sound in the room. I couldn't help it, okay. The idea of Justina holding the tablet in front of Gerard's comatose face was terrible. And yet, I couldn't stop laughing.

Kingsley's sharp squeak made me look at him. The little rat was telling me off on behalf of Gerald who half glared, half... I wasn't sure. He kind of looked amused, but I couldn't quite tell through the tears that were now in my eyes.

"It's good to see you laugh, Devon," Mary said as Justina sat at her desk and put the tablet onto its stand. "You've been so serious for such a long time."

Sobering slightly, I winked at Gerard before moving closer and taking his hand. Kingsley waited for me on the edge of his shoulder.

Offering my palm, I kissed my little best friend as he jumped onto it. He ran up my arm and snuggled into the crease of my neck as I turned my attention back to my boss.

"I'm assuming there's something you need to tell us." Justina waved at Mary when she didn't stop staring at Gerard.

My mirth threatened to erupt again. What was it about him that made Mary go weak at the knees? Yes, he was Mr Cool Guy. Mr Tattoo Handsome Man. But, he was also quite normal. Sort of. Maybe I was being unrealistic. Ever since we'd admitted how we felt about each other, we had lived in a state of fluffy feelings. When in reality, our shit still simmered underneath. It wasn't long ago that Gerard was adding his kills up to avenge his best friend.

"Yes, sorry, dear," Mary said, chuckling to herself. "I can't help it. Gerard reminds me of my husband when we first met."

My heart flickered as Mary turned her attention to Justina. Sharing a look with Gerard, I smiled as we both softened, our gaze relaxing. She had shared her story with us. We knew the guilt and blame she carried. I had so often preached to Gerard about blame. In turn, he had switched it back on me. If we had both agreed to stop blaming ourselves for accidents, or things that were out of our control, we couldn't blame each other. I hoped Mary would one day see that for herself too.

"I need some help with the stones. I need to prepare them for the solstice. If I don't set the ritual up in advance, there's a risk that Devon won't be disconnected from the warlock link. Or, even worse. The link could disintegrate altogether, which means..."

Her sentence trailed off, but we all knew what she was talking about. I hadn't really stopped to contemplate what would happen if that happened. I would die. The warlocks would become human. Their magic lost forever. Well, sort of. The impure magic would still be in the earth, just not accessible to those aboveground.

"What do you need from us?" Kurt came around the desk to talk to Mary.

Her face brightened as he came into view. "Oh, congratulations, my dear. I'm so pleased you're going to be a father. You better be a little more patient with the wee lad than you... oops."

Our jaws had dropped open in unison. Shit. Mary had just given away the sex of Justina's baby. What would the couple do? If it was me, I would probably be a little pissed. I loved surprises.

Gerard's fingers squeezed mine. I looked away from the others as they stared at each other, grins spreading on their face.

Pointing at his arm, Gerard said. "If Mary ever spills the beans about our kid, she might become number-"

Placing a hand over his lips, I stopped him from speaking. I would not have a number or tattoo mentioned in the same sentence as my child. Our child. Was he serious? He wanted to have children with me? They would be the weirdest kind of kids, considering our genes, but it would be fun to be a proper family. My little heart pattered all over the place as we gazed at each other.

Taking my hand, he pulled it away. "Well, that's if we ever have kids, of course. We don't know where life will take us next. What with..." Waving his hand towards my mother, he shrugged.

Andddd... he'd just ruined it. All my fuzzy feelings plummeted to the pit of my stomach. Mr Kind of Romantic had some things to learn.

"You, at the back," Mary called. "We need your input."

Jumping to attention, I let go of Gerard's hand and went to sit in my favourite leather chair. Justina and Kurt were staying professional, their quick glances easily covered by their stern faces. I hoped they were happy with the revelation. It really would suck if they'd decided to wait to find out.

"What do you need from us?" Justina was poised with her pen and paper, ready to take action.

Mary rubbed a hand over her face. The stress was obviously getting to her. She had said that she wouldn't get involved, but unfortunately, she'd been roped into my little problem.

"I need two things. Protection. If Bradley turns up again, I want to be safe from him while I go about my business. I also need some magic."

"Magic?" Kurt said. "What would a seer need with magic? You're an advisor."

It was amazing how Kurt could get away with saying something that would sound offensive coming from anyone else. Mary didn't even batter an eyelash as she leant forward. "I need the stones to remain pure until the solstice. I can cleanse them when you're here, but I'll need you to put a ward around them so Bradley cannot tamper with them."

That would take some magic. Oh boy. There was a lot of sinking feelings going on in my short arse body.

"Without knowing where Bradley's getting the new magic from, it's going to take a hell of a spell to keep that place protected." Justina eyed me, a small frown forming on her forehead.

All eyes turned to me as I tucked my feet onto the chair, hugging my knees to my chest. Every single person in the room knew about my addiction. A tiny bubble of heat made my skin burn as I thought about their double standards. One minute, they wanted me to stop using magic. The next, they demanded I help them with tons of it.

"I…"

"No." My father put his hand up, wagging his finger as he shook his head. "Devon's not in a position to keep using a high amount of magic. I've asked her to take it down a notch or two."

Putting my head in my hands as my muscles started to shake, I took a deep breath. A hand came to my back, rubbing gently. When I looked up, I was surprised to see my father there. Wow. He really did have my back. Literally.

"I think I need to do this, Dad." Grabbing his hand, I held tight. "But, if you're there with me, maybe you can help? Mum can back me up so it's not as much going directly through me."

The slow blink of his eyes made a lump come to my throat. He was concerned for me. For some reason, his worry made me feel stronger. I could beat it, my addiction. I could, and I would.

Moving to join us, my mother wrapped an arm around my father's waist. Tucking her hand into the hem of the belt around his blue jeans, she smiled up at him. "We can be there to support our girl. If she doesn't let go of the warlock link, she'll most certainly be swallowed by the addiction disease."

"How can...?" I coughed as I choked on my words. "How can I stay a magical person if I have an addiction? Alcoholics, drug addicts, gamblers, they have to stay away from their crutch at all times to overcome it."

My hands were shaking as I let go of my dad and stared down at them. It hadn't hit me until a moment ago how serious it was.

"I can help," Kurt piped up.

He glanced at Justina. She nodded before she stood. Coming over, she knelt in front of me.

My parents moved away, their views made known. I was centre of attention, yet again.

"As you know, I once had an addiction. Kurt helped me through it. One of the differences between us and the humans is the ability to manipulate things that humans wouldn't even think of."

59

Huh? Either she was hinting at something my little brain couldn't take in, or the amount of magic I'd been working with had killed off some brain cells.

"How has that got anything to do with addictions?"

Flicking her tongue out to wet her lips, Justina looked me in the eye. "I was able to stop taking vampire blood."

Letting her words hang in the air, Justina waited to see if anyone else would react to her confession. They didn't. Which was good, otherwise I'd be tempted to defend my friend.

"You're not going to be able to completely stop using your magic. So, I've been talking to Kurt. He thinks he can come up with a healing spell to take away the high you get from using magic."

"Effectively taking away the one thing that compels me to use it." My gaze dropped to my hands where they were clenched in my lap.

My nails were bitten down to the quick. A habit I'd been prone to when stressed. It really didn't help when I had an itch. No nails equalled no scratching satisfaction.

"Devon," Justina whispered, forcing me to look at her. "You have to want to give up your addiction for the spell to work. If not, it won't. It's a little bit like hypnosis but much stronger."

In that moment, it was just me and her in the room. She had been through what I had. She knew what it was like to crave something that made you feel good. Even if it only lasted a moment before the crash brought you down.

The shuffle of Kingsley as he walked down my chest and sat on my lap caused tears to pop into my eyes. He looked up at me, his little head bobbing. What was he trying to tell me?

"I think he's grateful that you didn't make him your familiar." Justina laughed as she straightened up. "Think about it."

Leaving me to my thoughts, Justina moved back towards her desk. "Mary, we'll come up tomorrow and assist you in any way we can."

Nodding once, Mary waved before she shut her Skype down. The room fell silent, no one uttering a word as the atmosphere grew heavy.

"I'll do it," I blurted, shocking everyone into looking at me.

Tilting her head to the side, Justina put her hands on her hips. "Do what exactly?"

Looking at Gerard, I gave him a smile. Without looking away, I spoke to my boss. "I'll do the spell tomorrow. I'll make it impossible for anyone to stop our attempt at getting this warlock link out of me. Then, once it's gone, Kurt can cast the spell on me so I can end my addiction to magic. I just want to go back to being a little bit normal again."

Kurt's scoff was joined by a bark of laughter from my mother. Justina didn't say a word, but I heard her getting back into her chair. I was ready to let go. Gerard had made me promise to live without magic for a week after I was disconnected, but I would prove to him that I didn't need the extra power at all. He could make me feel good. Although, fuck it, it wasn't about that. I had to learn to make myself feel good. If I couldn't make myself happy, no other bugger would be fit for the job.

6

"Do you believe I can do it?" I asked Gerard as we sat on the bench facing the river Thames.

The sun had set an hour ago. A breeze wafted from the water, sending the front of my hair away from my face. It was like a warm caress.

Mr Quiet Guy turned to look at me. Taking my hand, he brought it to his lips and kissed my knuckles. "Yes, I do. Devon, what I said in the bathroom-"

"Guys?!" Kurt shouted from the agency's front door. "We've got a lead we need to follow. Now."

Argh. Didn't Kurt know that my emotions were flipping all over the place? Today had been a heavy day, why couldn't I just enjoy the riverside view with my man? And, then ravish him in bed in the not too distant future?

Gerard switched into agent mode straight away. He'd only been awake for two days, but he was desperate to get back into the field. Mackenzie now had a big X on his head. Not only from the government but from my man. No one threatened the people he loved and got away with it. Although, maybe that was something we needed to talk about. Everyone in existence would want to threaten me if they knew what was going on with me. I was a freak of nature in so many ways.

"Wait, can't you finish what you were going to say?" I pleaded, grabbing the back pocket of his jeans and attempting to stop him from walking away. "We're not technically on duty."

The smirk on Gerard's face made me want to extend a fist and wipe it cleanly off. Alas, he was too pretty to actually carry out my inner threat.

"We're never off duty, are we? We'll pick up this conversation again soon."

Watching his tight arse, clad in black jeans, walk away from me, I resisted the urge to call out. To force him to face me. My heart hoped so hard that his foray into near death had made him see... what exactly? How much I meant to him? How he couldn't let me go?

Sighing, I dragged my size fours to the building. Once in the hallway, I waited, my shoulders slumped. I hadn't even had my gushy reunion with my man. Nothing had been resolved. And yet, he threw me a little wink when the others gathered. I couldn't wait to get his clothes off again.

"Devon, I have no idea what you're fantasising right now, but could you stop?" Justina's expression was hard.

I was about to raise my hands in apology, but she shut me down with a dismissive wave of her hand. "I've just had a call from a witch who frequents nightclubs in London. One of his human friends died from a magic drug overdose last week."

Oh, exciting. My stomach started to flutter at the prospect of work. I might complain about interruptions to my alone time with Mr Winky. Seriously, did he have something in his eye? But, I loved following the trail of a suspect. Or, at least getting intel from my very intense boss.

"He's just interrupted a deal with a man that matches Mackenzie's description.

65

Apparently, our informant has taken it upon himself to make sure no one else suffers the same fate of his friend."

"Shame there's not three hundred of him," I quipped. "They could police all the clubs in London."

Nope. They were not in the mood. Serious mode was well and truly switched on. Mentally chastising myself, I turned my own agent head on.

"Devon, Gerard, when we get to the club, I want you to speak to the owner. Find out if he's aware of drugs being sold in his club. Play nice. I don't want to offend anyone. We're going to question the man who made the report. He's hanging around outside the venue."

There was no need to reply or react. We knew our duty, we were ready. Reaching for Gerard, I froze when Kurt caught my elbow in mid-air.

"Hold back on the magic. The last thing we need is an addict to get trigger-happy for no reason."

I didn't have time to think about being offended before Gerard grabbed my wrist and relocated us to the club. The small line of people who waited by the door didn't notice us appear.

"Ignore Kurt." Gerard almost dragged me through the people to the front of the queue.

Showing his agency ID card, he nodded when the bouncer gestured for us to go in. The intoxicating vibration of music entered my aura as soon as we were in the small hallway that led to the inner sanctum of the dance club.

"Once this is over," I said, forcing Gerard to let go of me so I could straighten my top and wrap my fingers around my dagger handle. "I'm going out on the razz. I'm so ready to get raving drunk."

Without agreeing or disagreeing, Gerard opened the doors so we could enter. The vibe was low key. The music was dancey, but it was a little too early to be banging. Several paranormal beings were spread throughout the room. A dancefloor was on the left. Several booths were on the right with a bar directly in front of us.

"The bar." Gerard didn't wait for a reply as we strode across the room.

I'd only just heard his voice over the noise, which meant that we needed to interview the owner away from the premises, if he was here at all.

My spine tingled as I passed a vampire. His eyes traced the length of me, his tongue flicking out to press against his extended canine. As if I would be interested in a vampire.

Not bothering to make eye contact with him, I pushed through a couple of humans who were dancing on the walkway. Why did humans do that? There was a dancefloor for a reason.

"What can I get you?" the bartender shouted when Gerard leant over the sticky surface.

Placing my hand on it, I quickly pulled away. I couldn't exactly be judgemental about the place, considering my room at the agency was cluttered with tons of rubbish. It was about time I moved out and got my own place. At least no one, meaning Justina, would cringe every time they came to see me.

"The owner." Gerard flashed his badge at the same time as a man came out from a door beside the bar.

Waving us over, he opened the door and disappeared. The guard out front must have let him know that we'd arrived. Going over, we retraced his steps, following him down a hallway and into an office.

"Let me do the talking," Gerard said, softening his agent blow with a waist squeeze.

Er. No. I wasn't a damsel in distress agent. I was Devon Jinx. Kickass warrior princess. Okay, so I was exaggerating just a little.

"Who are you? What can I do for you?" The man was dressed in a pink shirt and very skinny white jeans.

"Sorry for barging in on you, but we've just had a tipoff about drugs being dealt in your premises. Would you know anything about that?" Gerard's feet were evenly apart, firm on the red carpeted floor.

My gaze traced the sex swing in the corner, my mouth only just staying closed.

"I'm Jack, nice to meet ya," the owner said in a thick cockney accent. "And, who might you sexy motherfuckers be?"

There weren't many men that phased me, but Jack was a character. His charisma was matched by the outlandish pictures on the walls. He lowered himself behind his mahogany desk as he lifted a box from a drawer. Taking out a cigar, he offered one to Gerard.

Ignoring him, Gerard flashed his card again. "We're from the Hunted Witch Agency. We're after a man called Mackenzie Bruce and a woman called Candy Fieldman. Have you seen either of them tonight?"

Cocking his head to the side, Jack chewed on the end of his cigar. "I know Candy. Intimately, if you know what I mean."

For some reason, he was speaking to me. I didn't care about his sexual endeavours. Although, I was a little gobsmacked by him, so I stayed quiet. Gerard had ordered me to let him take the lead.

"Have they been at the club tonight?" Stepping forward, Gerard leant on the desk, his broad shoulders crowding Jack.

"I know you!" the man suddenly exclaimed, getting up from his seat and pointing at me. "You're the bitch who tried to break into this club, months ago."

A blast from the past battered my brain. Of course. Jeremy, the witch Gerard had killed, had forced me to try and gain access to the club. Although, we had managed, to be fair.

"I thought I recognised this place," I said, absentmindedly.

"I've got a good mind to ring my mate, Trygger."

A grin came to my face as Gerard looked between us. "I've not seen Thunder Hunter in a while. Go ahead."

Jack paused with his hand hovering over his phone. "Ah, you know the bastard. No point in getting him involved then. What the fuck do you want with Mackenzie and Candy? And, no, before you ask again, I've not seen them tonight. I've been in here... waiting."

"Waiting for what, exactly?"

I almost slapped my forehead. Asking that question had made Jack smirk to himself. It was obvious that he was probably waiting for something that I didn't even want to think about.

"Just some friends. We've decided to test the swing to see how many people we can fit on it."

Gerard's arm muscles tightened. "How often do you see Candy in these premises? We have reason to believe they're poisoning magic drugs that are being sold around London. Do you know anything about it?"

Leaning back in his chair, Jack put his legs up onto the desk. The smoke from his cigar wafted around his head as he breathed it out. "Nah, mate, I'm a pretty open guy, but I ain't a fool. My bouncers are witches. They check everyone for magic before they're allowed in the club. I ain't got the money to fight big lawsuits if something goes wrong. You know what I mean?"

If Thunder Hunter, the grandson of Thor, was best friends with Jack, I knew that he would probably be telling the truth. Although I didn't have much experience with the man who was a warrior, I knew that he was honourable. Well, kind of.

"How about Cameron Fieldman? Do you have any connections with him?" Gerard stood straight and cracked his knuckles.

It was a little amusing to watch my man try to intimidate the un-intimidateable Jack. They were miles apart from each other, but each one had his own power. Jack might be human but apparently he knew people. Not many humans would be able to persuade witches to work for them.

"I know Cameron through the circuit, but I'm not personally associated with him. I've heard some dodgy things. And, I have too many dodgy things going on in my own world. Although, completely legal, of course." Winking at me, Jack offered me his lit cigar.

My instant reaction was to cringe. There was no way in hell I would smoke a cigar that had been in his mouth. Was that cruel? Maybe. Was he creepy? A little. Was I shocked for the first time in ages? Definitely.

"What dodgy things have you heard?"

Ignoring Gerard, Jack got up from his seat. Coming around the desk, he looked down at me. "You're awfully quiet for someone who's got all that magic sizzling inside. Devon Jinx, I'd like to feel some of your inside-"

Before I could reply, Gerard's hand shot in front of my face. His fingers wrapped around Jack's throat, squeezing tight.

"Firstly, you're lucky she doesn't use that magic to cut off your dick. Secondly, she's mine."

The club owner's eyes bulged as his cheeks blossomed dark red. If Mr Protective Hunky Bad Cop didn't let go soon, he would kill the man.

Grabbing Gerard's elbow, I ran my hand down his tattooed arm. As my fingers reached his wrist, he let go, dropping Jack to his feet.

"Well," Jack choked. "That wasn't very friendly, mate."

Keeping my expression calm when Gerard looked at me, I indicated that we should leave with a nod of my head. The huge bubble of excitement that sat a little lower than my stomach distracted me. Gerard had never been so macho over me before. I liked it. He could beat men who made passes at me all the time if I got to watch. Hmm... maybe that wasn't a healthy thing to fanaticise about. Although, not many men bothered, so it didn't matter. They could probably tell that I was trouble from ten thousand miles away.

"Before you leave," Jack said as we moved towards the door. "I promise that I'll keep an eye out for Candy. If she turns up, I'll call you."

Nodding our thanks, we made our way outside. The adrenaline in my veins was compounded by the heady dance music. I wanted to take Gerard to an alley and jump him. Alas, Justina and Kurt met us as soon as we walked out of the door.

"Anything?" Kurt snapped, clearly not in a jovial mood.

"No. You?" Gerard's curt reply made me roll my eyes.

Men were so...

"Cheer up, boys," Justina said. "We've just found out that Candy was the one trying to sell the drugs. Mackenzie was tagging along, looking like a lost sheep. And..." Pulling an evidence bag out of her pocket, she grinned at me.

The corners of Gerard's eyes creased as he spotted the syringe. It was full. My own smile spread as I clapped her on the shoulder. "Good job!"

"Excuse me," someone interrupted us. "Isn't that the woman you're looking for?"

The bouncer was pointing down the street. Candy, her dark hair tied in a ponytail, was laughing with another girl. They were outside the kebab shop, the light from the window highlighting her as she took a swig from a beer bottle. Did the girl have no conscience?

All four of us started to sprint as soon as Mackenzie came out of the shop holding a bag. Kurt was in front, Gerard almost beside him. Justina was next, me last. Of course. It had nothing to do with the fact that I wasn't as fit as them, it was because of my little legs. That was my excuse, and I wouldn't change it.

"Hey!" Kurt shouted when Mackenzie dropped his bag and grabbed Candy.

They started to run, looking over their shoulders as we got closer to them. My boots pounded the concrete, trying to keep up with the others.

As we were passing the kebab shop, Candy's friend reached out and grabbed my arm. Spinning back to her, I flicked my dagger out of my jacket. Using my momentum, I thrust it forward, aiming it straight in her face. She cowered back, her arms coming up to protect her head. She was human. Shit.

"Oi! You can't do that!" someone shouted as they came out of the kebab shop.

Waving my hand, I cast a memory spell over them both before heading off to catch up with the others. They had come to a stop at the end of the street, their huffing the only sign they'd been running at all.

"Disappeared?" I asked as I tucked my dagger away.

"No," Kurt said, running a hand through his shaggy hair. "We caught them. They're standing right there. Can't you see them?"

Flipping him off, I rolled my eyes as Gerard took my hand. He smiled down at me, his eyebrows raised. "It was a stupid question, D."

Oh, that was a new one. A smile came to my lips. "I like that."

His gaze locked on mine as the others chattered about going back to the agency. Our breath deepened, the world shrinking to evolve around us.

"You like the nickname D?"

He tilted his head to the side, coming closer as he stroked my thumb. Biting my bottom lip, I nodded as I smiled.

"Oh jeez." Justina sighed. "Do you remember when we were like that? The rush of adrenaline used to get our blood pumping, and we couldn't keep our hands off each other."

The moment was ruined. Breaking eye contact with my man, I frowned at the pair as they watched us. If Justina was talking about their personal relationship, the pregnancy must be effecting her hormones.

"That's not something I need to know about," I said, laughing when Kurt wiggled his eyebrows at me.

"Oh, come on. We're all grown up. How do you think I put a baby in there?" He pointed at Justina's stomach.

Batting his hand away, Justina looked horrified. Her mouth dropped open as Kurt tried to placate her, albeit with a shrug.

"Okaaayy," I said, tugging on Gerard's hand. "We all need a good night's sleep. Shall we get back?"

"Pfft," Kurt snorted. "Just don't keep us awake all night with your 'sleeping'."

As we flashed back to the agency, I couldn't help but wonder if this new family was as dysfunctional as my own.

7

"You look like you're walking funny, Devon," Kurt called as we headed into the clearing of Clava Cairns.

My fingers itched to throw a spell of badness towards him. Something gross. Like dog poo right in front of his shoe, just before it hit the ground.

"She is walking funny," Mary said as she linked arms with Gerard.

Okay, I might be a bit jumpy, but it wasn't because we'd been up all night, which we had... it was because the magic of both warlock and witch energy was trying to push into me. I'd been avoiding it as much as I could, almost going cold turkey over the last day or two. I was twitchy. Addict twitchy.

"Okay," Justina interrupted before any unsavoury discussions could start. "I've cleared the energy that was here. It's gone for now, but I'm not sure how long it will stay gone. Like I say, it's not a magic I recognise."

"We better get on with it then." Mary almost shoved Gerard towards the main stone. "I sent you the memo of what we'd need."

Kurt grunted as he unloaded the satchel from his shoulder. "Candles, salt, sand. Enough to build the foundation of a house."

Waving his remarks away, Mary glared at me. "And you?"

Releasing the air from my lungs, I took the dagger out of my pocket. "One Essex dagger. This is my baby, okay? Please don't do anything to harm it."

Holding out her hand, she pursed her lips without saying anything. There was no point in being teenagery about it. She had to use the dagger to prepare for the unlinking in three days' time.

Slipping my beloved dagger handle onto her palm, I stuck my bottom lip out. Not having my baby with me made me feel naked.

Shuffling to the middle of the group as we gathered around, she handed the dagger to Kurt. "You're going to have to cast the preparation spell. Justina would've been the one to do it, but now that she's with child, we can't risk it. I requested that Devon's parents stay behind because too much magic will hurt the area. I need agents who will fight if there's a threat."

Kurt's face was serious as he took the weapon. His eyes widened slightly before he tucked it into his own pocket. Probably couldn't handle the power it possessed. Or, maybe he was icked out by the fact that it had been close to my body. Either way, I missed the dagger already.

"Gerard, Kurt," Justina said, holding up her tablet and scanning it around the area for the seventh time. "If you could run the sand and salt around the perimeter of the clearing, I'll watch out for any interference."

The men grunted but set to work instantly, chatting amongst themselves. Justina stood in the middle of the clearing, spinning slowly. Her tablet beeped every now and then, usually when it passed me. Yes, my energy was strong enough to cause an electronic reaction. Now that was something I could put on my CV. Just in case the agency ever kicked me out, which they better not. I wouldn't know what to do without my new family.

"Okay, so, Devon," Mary started, pointing to the main stone. "You're going to use this powerful energy portal to transfer the link. On solstice, the portal will open at exactly midnight. The reason we need to prep the area now is so that no one can steal the warlock magic when the moon hits the apex and you touch the stone."

My palms grew damp at the idea of the link leaving me. It was good. It really was good. It would be fine. I wouldn't die. I would stay alive. And, I would be kickass without the extra magic.

Mary tucked her long grey hair behind her ear. "It's natural to be nervous, wee one." Taking my hand, she wiped away the perspiration. "You've tasted the nectar of what magic can be. But, you've lost yourself in the process. Time to get you back."

Swallowing, I dropped my head, tears coming to my eyes as my chest squeezed. "Thank you," I whispered.

Slapping my hand, Mary brought me back to attention. "Buck up, half-breed," she sang. "Let's get to it."

Pointing at the stone, she indicated that I join her right next to it. "Once the protection spell is up, you and Kurt will stand side by side, just here." Taking my waist, she pushed me to face the stone head on.

It was quite a flat stone, considering how tall it was. But, there was something mesmerising about it. Something powerful.

Mary chattered on. "Kurt will cast the blood spell."

"Blood spell?" I almost choked.

Placing her hands on her hips, Mary frowned. "Of course. How else do you think we can keep you here? When the link goes, you'll stay in this clearing. You do need to decide where to send it first."

"Oh, shit."

Yeah, Mary had asked me to speak to Maxwell about that. It may have slipped my mind considering Gerard had been in a coma, and Mackenzie had escaped prison.

"You know what's on the top of your priorities list then, don't you? Otherwise, you'll have a ton of ex-warlocks ready to completely annihilate you. And, quite frankly, I wouldn't blame them."

Turning away to walk around the stone, Mary muttered to herself. I tuned her out as I stared. She was right. Of course she was. If

I let my scatterbrain run amok much longer, every paranormal creature in the world would come looking for me for some reason or another.

"So, the blood spell," I said, following Mary as she walked around. "Is there anything I need to do?"

Nodding, the seer grasped my hand in hers and placed it on the stone. "Yes. Your hand will be covered in blood. It must go here as soon as Kurt has sliced your palm. He will repeat the spell three times to connect to the earth, the sun and the moon."

"You know a lot about witch magic considering you're a seer."

Letting me go, she grinned to herself. "Oh, I've seen more than you can even imagine in your mind. More than your whole lifetime will encounter. Be grateful that you get to contain your own experience to yourself and those around you. Being able to see what's going to happen to everyone else is a tough burden."

I didn't doubt her, not one bit. It was hard enough to figure out what I was going to eat for dinner, let alone everything she had to decide. A seer had a moral obligation to help those in danger when they came to them. If they had seen the outcome, they couldn't tell a person, but they could guide them. The responsibility would send me over the edge.

"Once the blood spell links you to the stone, you'll be the only one able to control the portal when it opens." Justina made me jump as she came to stand next to me. "We will leave it alone, with the strong barrier spell around the clearing, until the solstice. I'll have a magical surveillance ward set up by the gated entrance."

Kurt strode over to us as he rubbed his sandy hands on his jeans. "All done. Let's get the circle done. The candles are in place. All lit. We just need two more witches to perform the spell."

Movement commenced as we all walked to a candle. There were four of them, spaced quite far apart. I almost couldn't see Kurt as he went behind one of the cairns.

Four candles was an odd number. Well no, actually, it was even. But, still, it wasn't often used in the spells I'd cast. Not that I'd done any traditional witch magic for a while. I would probably have to go back to practicing once I was disconnected from the ley line. A weird excitement made the tips of my fingers tingle as I thought about that.

Reaching my allotted place, I turned to face the centre of the clearing. We had agreed an exact time to start chanting the barrier spell. The others were going to put in as much magic as I was. I wasn't going to use anything more than I would have if I was a normal witch. A normal witch. Me, a normal witch? The hassles of my current life would fade away. It would be refreshing to not worry about anything other than whether the next bastard I was hunting was getting away.

My phone beeped on the hour. Holding my arms to the side, I glanced at Mary to check all was well. She was holding Justina's techy tablet, moving around in a slow circle to watch for danger. Apparently, my boss had turned the sound up so we could hear it if it went off. Mary wouldn't be able to do anything to protect us, so we had to know if there was a threat.

"Here goes," I muttered as I started the spell.

The small sound of my voice disappeared as the flame on the candle in front of me rose higher, almost scorching my face. Shit, we were a powerful foursome. *No, brain, no. Just no.* Why did my brain instantly go to inappropriate thoughts?

The other flames around the clearing were as high as mine. That was good. I didn't want to be putting too much energy into the spell. My feet were warm, but in a nice way, not the heat that attacked my nerve endings.

Just as we were about to finish the spell, Justina's tablet burst into high frequency beeps. Shit, there was an intruder. Rushing away from the flame, towards the inner circle, I looked around for the others. They were on their way, instantly heading to the centre.

By the entrance, the shape of Bradley loomed. He suddenly leapt over the wooden gate, his tiny frame speeding towards us.

Reaching into my pocket, I froze. Kurt had my dagger. And, he was currently half way across the clearing. Oh boy. We all knew that I wasn't any good at hand to hand combat. Being so close to the entrance, I was the one nearest our enemy.

"Mary!" I shouted. "Get in there!" Pointing at the cairn next to the stone, I planted my feet on the ground, ready to defend the others. If I had to use my magic, so be it.

Doing as she was told, the seer went inside the built up circle of stones and ducked down. The roof had worn away a long time ago, leaving her vulnerable, but at least she was out of sight.

"Devon Jinx," the male seer called. "I have a message for you!"

My arms flicked out to the side as warlock magic poured into me. The flames licked my skin, enticing me to pull more. No, I had to keep control. I had the right amount to-

Something blasted past my shoulder, knocking me back. Pain burnt the skin that had been hit. Probably by a bullet. The little bastard, he'd drawn blood.

"Devon!" Gerard shouted. "Get to safety."

He wanted me to flash out of there?

Ignoring my man, I formed a ball of pink flames in my hands. The colour was tinged with red and black. That wasn't a good thing.

Bradley was closer, his arm extended. The gun he had fired was still aimed at me. "Your warlock magic is contaminated."

His shout made me pause. Was that the message?

My arm throbbed as the others approached. They held back, clearly seeing the threat. If Bradley fired, he could hit me. Although, the bullet probably wouldn't get through the ball of magic I was holding.

Everyone in the clearing stopped dead. The proof of what Bradley was saying was evident. The black that swirled in my magic

was new. I had never had that before. The only person I had seen-

"Vernon Jupiter sends his love." Flicking his hand in the air, Bradley pulled the trigger.

Although there was a lot of noise, my ears focused on the swish of the bullet as it flew towards me. Shoving the magic ball, I grunted as the heavy energy weighed me down. As soon as it left my arms, I jumped to the side to avoid the bullet. The pain that sliced through my thigh told me that I hadn't been successful. My arse collided with the grass, my bones rattling at the impact.

"Devon!" Gerard shouted.

Another gunshot rang out at the same time as my magic blasted into Bradley. He was hit by both, his small frame instantly crumbling to the floor.

Somehow scrambling to my feet, I hobbled to meet Gerard as he came to me. I opened my arms, ready to be hugged, but he grabbed the tops of my arms to check where I'd been hit. Boo. I wanted a hug.

"I'm okay. They're just flesh wounds."

Lifting the sleeve of my shirt, he nodded. "Yes, a graze here. However, your leg is pissing blood. We need Kurt to get the bullet out."

"Wait!"

He had gone to turn, but I tugged him back. "We need to finish the ritual."

"Don't be crazy."

His green eyes narrowed on me when I put my hands on my hips, almost falling over as the pain from the bullet in my thigh made my head pound. "We have to finish this! Especially if Vernon is somehow connecting to our world."

Kurt came over after making sure Bradley was dead. Justina was closing down the slit of magic that had opened by the entrance again.

"Get his body out of here," Mary called as she came out of the cairn. "Then finish the spell!"

My muscles started to shake uncontrollably. Gerard reached for me just as I stepped back. We had to finish the...

8

Gasping awake, I sat bolt upright. Kurt put a hand on my arm, forcing me to lie back down. The spell. Bradley. How did I get here?

"You lost a lot of blood." Kurt glanced around the infirmary. "But, I sorted you out."

Sorted me out? Was that code for something? The throb of the wound in my leg made me relax against the plush pillow.

"The ritual?" My stomach was heavy as I tried not to worry about the implications of what had happened.

Shaking his head, Kurt pulled his mixing table towards him. A bowl of red tincture was the only thing on it. Hopefully he'd healed me with his magic, although, the pain was still there, which meant that the bullet must have done some damage.

"All went well."

Huh? Had I just woken up in the twilight zone? What the hell was he talking about?

Smiling, he undone the dressing around my thigh. Blinking, I noticed that he'd cut my jeans. "Dude," I exclaimed. "These were my favourite pair!"

"Who gives a fuck about clothing? You were losing blood. I saved your life. You should be saying 'thank you, Kurt, you amazing man, you'."

Did he seriously just do an impression of me? High pitched voice and all?

A giggle escaped as my head fell back on the pillow. A sharp pain where he was working made me look up again. Teeth clenched, I watched as he peeled the dressing away. There were a fair few stitches.

"It went deep," Kurt said, obviously reading my expression. "I had to cut a fair bit."

"Nice." My stomach rolled slightly.

Picking up the bowl with the tincture, Kurt took the soaked dressing out and placed it on my wound. I sucked in a breath as heat pulsed, making the wound on my leg feel tight.

"It's a bit of cayenne, ginger and ginkgo biloba. Mixed with a healing spell, of course.

It increases blood flow to the site of your stitches, quickening healing time to literally a day or two. How do you think I managed to get about so quickly after my legs were broken?"

Sighing, I looked up at the ceiling. I felt a little bit strange. As if my head was swirling.

"I gave you some opiate painkiller."

Kurt was seriously reading my mind.

"No, you're talking aloud. You have a habit of being weird when you're delirious."

"You don't say!" My brain cleared suddenly.

Holding a wand over my third eye, Kurt had whispered something. "There, the effects of the painkillers will still do their job, but your mind is no longer foggy. Can't stand you acting weird."

The thought of being offended slipped from my mind when I remembered the ritual. Kurt had said that it went well. That wasn't possible. I'd passed out before we could even get the protection spell up, let alone anything else.

About to open my mouth, I paused when Gerard strolled in, a box in one hand and Kingsley in the other.

Tears popped to my eyes as Kurt moved away to let Gerard sit next to me. Kingsley did a flying jump from Gerard's hand as soon as he was near the bed. My furry best friend ran up my good leg, then crossed over my stomach. Tickling the skin on my arm, he was light on his feet as he made his way up and onto my shoulder.

Stroking him, I laughed when he squeaked loudly. There was nothing like a Kingsley hug. Picking him up, I kissed his little head and stroked his back. He nudged me, asking for a biscuit.

"I don't have one, little fella," I whispered, feeling guilty for not spending more time with him.

"Here," Gerard said as he sat down. "I figured you'd greet him before me."

My gaze went to his, my heartbeat relaxing when he smiled and handed me a biscuit. He knew me well. Not that I didn't love them both equally. Actually, that was bull. Kingsley won every time.

"I love you, too." I laughed, putting Kingsley on my lap so he could eat his treat.

Leaning his elbows on the bed, Gerard put his chin in his hands as he looked up at me. "You're so pretty."

A bolt of fizzling excitement rushed through me. Why was he being complimentary? He was never-

"Oh, yeah, that was my next job," Kurt said. "I'm going to update Justina so I'll let you take care of it."

What? Bringing my hand up to my face, I cringed when my fingers traced something dried on. "I still have splatters of my own blood over me?"

A tide of anger tried to ride up my chest, but I released it through a breath. I wasn't cross with Kurt, he had saved my leg. But, Bradley was a bastard for drawing blood in the first place.

"The ritual!" I said again, frustrated that I was getting so easily distracted. "What happened? Is Bradley dead?"

Nodding, Gerard got up and retrieved a bowl of water. Coming back, he sat down and soaked a cloth in it.

"Both your magic and my bullet killed him." Brushing my hair away from my face, Gerard started to rub my cheeks, cringing when he glanced at the bright red blood residue left on the cloth.

His touch was tender, yet deliberate. He didn't want to hurt me, but he wouldn't be too gentle. He needed to get the job done. It was basically his whole persona. It was no wonder I loved him. A man who was tough enough to reach his goals, but kind enough to soften a blow.

"Kurt said the ritual went well. What was he talking about?"

Gerard's neck flushed with a light pink as he avoided my gaze, his concentration completely enraptured on cleaning my face.

"Tell me!" My patience was wearing thin.

Kingsley turned three times on the sheet that covered my top half before settling on my good thigh. He knew important stuff was going on near my shoulder.

Clearing his throat, Gerard sat back and dropped the cloth in the bowl. "There, all clean."

"You weren't complimenting me at all. And, there I thought you'd turned a new leaf." My smile was joined by the slight raise of my eyebrows.

Shrugging, Gerard winked before turning serious. "Your mother joined us at the clearing."

Ah, good, he was going to tell me exactly what had happened. Hopefully they had found a way to finish it without me, although that kind of seemed impossible.

"We then..." Gerard almost choked on his words. "...don't get angry, but Kurt had tied a tourniquet around your thigh. Mary kept a close eye on you while we finished the protection spell."

Why would I get angry at them?

He must have read the question in my gaze because he ducked his head and spoke quickly. "We then stood you up, me holding you for support. Kurt did the spell, cut your hand and held it against the stone. It was the best we could do in the circumstances."

Keeping my face as straight as I possible could, I didn't let out the humour that wanted to escape. I could milk his guilt for all it was worth. When he looked up at me, a weary expression on his face, I burst out laughing. Who was I kidding? I'd never been able to hide how I was feeling. I was way too much of an unhinged female.

"That's pretty genius, if you ask me. Did it work?"

Sitting back, his shoulders relaxed, his tattoos moving as he handed me the box he'd brought in with him. "Yes, it did."

"What's this?" Gerard had never bought me a gift before.

Narrowing my gaze on him as I held the box in my hand, I tried not to get excited. Stemming the rush of girly emotions that threatened to overwhelm me, I swallowed hard.

"It's just something little, don't get too excited. I made it just before we went to Scotland, before we fell out."

"Fell out? Does that mean we've made up?"

Sitting forward, Gerard gestured for me to open the box. My fingers itched to rip the paper off, but we needed to have the conversation we'd been avoiding since Gerrard had come out of the coma.

"Please," he muttered. "Then we'll talk."

Butterflies flapped in my stomach as I opened the packaging. Not many people brought me presents. Certainly not Mr Dishy Agent Man.

My thumbs were clumsy as I wrenched the top of the box open, gasping when I saw what was inside.

"The little git only just stayed still long enough for me to get it." Gerard stroked Kingsley's head where he rested on my thigh.

Picking out the small slab of clay, I instantly sucked in a sob. Footprints of my rat had been embedded into it. It was moulded into a heart shape, a small hole drilled through the top. Kingsley's name was etched underneath the four paw prints.

"What do you think?" Gerard was sitting on the edge of his seat, his handsome face concerned.

Grinning, I reached forward, cringing when the stitches in my leg pulled. "Come here."

He moved so I didn't have to cause myself pain. Our lips met, crushing together as I tried to stop the tears that threatened.

Taking his lips away, Gerard leant his forehead against mine. "Devon, I... I don't want to lose you."

"You won't," I whispered back. "I told you, I'm going to give up the ley line."

"That means you're going to give up everything for me. How do we know that we're always going to feel the same way?"

He gazed into my eyes, trying to read my soul. My heartbeat increased as a flash of fear crossed his face. I had never seen Mr Hard Exterior look afraid. Of anything.

"Life happens. People get together, they break up. But we have a little more staying power, don't you think? Most paranormals stick together longer. Something about how we're wired. Humans used to be the same, but they've lost that dedication to growth. They now go after shallow instant gratification. There's no depth. But, us?

We're much more complex. Our powers or abilities make us look at ourselves more closely. To understand who we are so we can control them. It helps us relate to another person easier. To not give up on them as soon as they trigger us."

"Who are you?" Gerard whispered with a smile as he kissed me on the nose, then the cheek, then the lips. "Your wisdom precedes you Devon Jinx."

Cupping his cheek, I flicked out my tongue, just catching the end of his nose. "There, I'm back again. Thank you for my gorgeous present."

"You're welcome." Sitting back in his seat, Gerard took my hands. "So… what next?"

Leaning my head back against the pillow, I sighed. "After I'm rid of the warlock link, I'll speak to my mother. I'm not sure how I get disconnected from the ley line, but it will have to be fairly soon. Otherwise, the agent at Paranormal MI5 will come knocking."

Rubbing a hand over his face, Gerard yawned. "Sorry," he said, shaking himself. "I didn't sleep. Kurt wouldn't let me in while he did your stitches. Are you really sure you want to do this?"

The bags under his eyes were bigger than usual. My man had lost sleep over me. Cute.

Although, I had basically played vigil by his bedside when he was in a coma, so he owed me at least one night. And a fry up.

"Yes, I'm certain. I've gone over it several times in my brain. And, as you know, my brain is quite small, so it didn't take too long to decide."

My gaze narrowed on him as he nodded. He wasn't supposed to agree with me. Although, he wasn't supposed to placate me with denials either. No wonder men didn't know what women wanted. I didn't really know myself. Except, I did. I wanted Gerard. I wanted my agency family. I wanted a family of my own. Eventually.

"I love you." His statement would've been romantic had he not yawned again.

My laughter filled the room as he surged from his chair and shut me up with a kiss. One that quickly deepened.

The sound of the door opening made us pull apart. Gerard grinned at me as my parents hurried in, their faces tight with worry. My mother's mouth was pinched as she rushed over, almost shoving Gerard out of the way.

I smiled at my man, knowing full well that we'd decided that no matter what, we would stick together. I loved him too. I'd never wanted to be with someone the way I did him. And, if it meant I had to give up my heritage because of that, so be it. He was more important to me than my magic.

"Thank goodness you're okay," my mother gushed as she tucked a stray strand of hair behind my ear.

"Look what Gerard made me." I almost gloated as I held up the love heart and grinned.

My parents exchanged a look as Gerard muttered a goodbye and headed off to get some sleep. Why had they frowned? Oh...

"Justina hasn't been able to trace Vernon Jupiter." My father quickly changed the subject.

My mother still frowned, her fingers tracing a symbol of some sort on the cover over me. She wasn't going to let it go as easily as he was.

"The longer you put it off, the harder it will be." Her face, similar to mine, was drawn, the lines around her eyes thickened slightly.

Being back had probably increased her stress levels ten-fold. Maybe they should go into retirement. That wasn't a very nice thought. They weren't exactly old enough for that. However, my skin burned at her suggestion.

101

"I don't think this is the time to be-"

My father was cut off by my mother's hand abruptly raising in front of his face. Woah, talk about passive aggressive. Or maybe it was just aggressive aggressive. Either way, I didn't want to get involved in their domestic.

"Devon has forgotten her duty." Coming closer, she perched on the edge of the bed. Her hair was tied up into a bun, her features nice and neat. Not like me. I was the messy version.

"I've not forgotten my duty, mum, I..." What could I say?

Now was not the time to tell her my plans. I had to get the warlock link sorted before I even thought about releasing the ley line. Telling my mother now would only cause tension.

Watching her hands as they squeezed together, my mother swallowed hard before she spoke. "I've found you a nice male witch who's descended from Essex lines. He has agreed to meet you for a potential match."

"You what?!" I roared, grabbing Kingsley as he jumped so high, he almost fell off the bed.

Instantly calming my temper so he wasn't scared, I tucked my best friend into the pocket of my shirt. I really needed a good shower and change of clothes. The poor boy would probably suffocate from my musky body.

Staring at the ground, my father shuffled his feet. Did he have anything to do with this? How could the people who had broken the law with their love arrange something so cold?

"You married for love. How dare you try and dictate who I marry! You're still connected to the ley line, even though you didn't marry an Essex witch."

Sliding off the bed, my mother slunk into the chair, her fingers drumming on the wooden arm. "I know. It's because of your grandmother. The ancestors needed someone stable to take care of our side. They allowed me to keep my role of protecting it."

"Well, you better cancel that meeting with the potential match. I've got far too much shit going on for you to even... Scrap that, just... leave me alone."

If my leg wasn't still healing under Kurt's magical gauze, I would've got up and marched out myself. Unfortunately, my parents stayed where they were, watching me.

"We did this to you," my father whispered, his eyes sorrowful as he ducked his head.

Rage flared within me, the heat of it burning my insides as I clenched my fists by my side. Kingsley pitter-pattered up my arm to sit in the crook of my neck. He rubbed his little head against my jaw, trying to calm the whirlwind of emotion inside me.

"No," I said through gritted teeth. "You didn't do this to me. You created me, yes. That was probably a mistake."

"Never!" My mother jumped up from her seat, her hand grabbing mine and squeezing hard. Almost too hard. "You are my pride and joy. I watch you with these people, see how you've become a part of their team. A professional." She coughed when I raised my eyebrows. "Most of the time."

"We made it hard for you," my father chimed up, coming closer. "That's what I meant. It was selfish of us to have you. We wouldn't change it, ever. But, I'm sorry that our love caused you so much grief."

Emotion flooded me. He was right. Being a half breed had made life a lot harder than it would've been if my mother had married another witch. However, she hadn't. She had married my father, and they had been very happy ever since. I was proud of them for standing up for their love. It would've been so much easier to push each other away and go with the rules. So why was my mother trying to force me to do what she wouldn't? It didn't make sense.

Tears dropped from my mother's eyes as she stroked my hair. "I don't want you to lose your birth right. Seeing you as a powerful woman, a powerful paranormal, makes my heart swell with pride. I don't want to see you struggle again."

"You believe that if I stay with Gerard, I'll be weak?"

The incline of her head told me all I needed to know. Where was the vehement denial?

"Let me tell you something," I said. "As a child, I grew up being bullied because you broke the law."

My father's cringe didn't make me feel guilty. I wouldn't hold back anymore. All the anxiousness, the pain, and the detachment since they'd returned, bubbled to the surface. I had to speak my truth.

"Devon," he started.

"No." Holding up my hand, I refused to let him speak. "It's my turn."

I gently pulled my hand away from my mum. She walked back until my father's arm came around her waist. It seemed he was her support, her rock. It was inspiring, and yet, I had to tell them how I felt.

Pulling myself up to sit straighter, I looked at them. "As a child, your love inspired me. I saw how much you cared for each other. The bullying, I could handle, because I could see why you'd gone against the rules."

They glanced at one another, their gazes softening slightly. Memories must have been circling through their minds, just like they were in mine. Happier times.

"But when you disappeared, my life shattered. Isaac Senior took me in, told me that you were probably dead. And, do you know what I concocted in my mind?"

They shook their heads, their attention fully on me.

"I believed that the government had finally caught up to you and issued you both the death penalty because you'd broken the law. Well, two laws actually. You'd married inter-species, and you'd produced a child. A half-breed."

Neither of them flinched at my words. Good. If they showed signs of weakness now, I would have to disown them. I needed them to see the point I was trying to make. But, they had to look at themselves for that to happen.

"Mother, you sacrificed your life for dad. You thought you'd lose the ley line link, but the ancestors let you keep it. It worked out well. I hated you."

The sudden change in topic finally got a reaction from them. My mother's eyebrows sank as her eyes filled with tears. My father swallowed, dropping my gaze for a second.

"You had left me. You had chosen each other, dragging me into your life too. Somehow you were still accepted, but only just. Theresa, the leader of the London coven, let you stay. You should've been the leader, but because of what you'd done, you were downgraded."

The thoughts and feelings I'd had in my mind since I was ten years old came spewing out like verbal diarrhoea. However, they tasted a little better than shit. Because they needed to be said.

"Okay, enough of the history lesson." I huffed, shaking my head. "Let me get to my point."

Nothing was said as I gathered myself. Perspiration lined my palms as I took a deep breath. "I've never forgiven you for leaving me. Firstly, even though I believed you were dead, I blamed you for everything. The reason you were dead was your fault. That's what my ten-year-old self thought. And then..." My throat closed as I remembered the day I had received the letter from my mother after fourteen years.

"And, then, we just flew straight back into your life." My father let go of my mother to come over to me.

I waved him away, unable to face physical contact when I wanted to break down. Tears were dribbling down my face as I breathed slowly. "Yes. You were suddenly alive, instantly there. It's taken some assimilating to get used to it. I'm grateful to have you back. Happy to see that you're still as in love now as you were then."

Their shared look was one of regret. Their sorrow evident in the creases around their mouths as they blinked slowly, heavily.

My father gripped his hands together as he looked at me. "That's what I meant when I said we'd caused all this. We weren't there to guide you. We left you, even though we thought we were protecting you from Helena."

Shaking my head, I swallowed my tears back. "When you left me," I said, stroking Kingsley when he squeaked for attention. "I was a child. Now, I'm an adult. I've made choices. I was a rebel as a teen, causing trouble in the witch world. I was careless about the warlock leadership. I joined the agency to try and... I dunno, fit in somewhere. You were not here. I'm old enough to make my own choices, which is why I'm here, with a bullet wound in my leg. Not because of you. Which means, I can also..."

My sentence trailed off when Gerard came in with a smile on his face. He came around the other side of the bed, a tray in his hand. He was seemingly oblivious to the fact that we were having a very serious conversation.

"Look," he gushed, picking up a plate. "I made you a fry up, and I didn't even burn anything."

I grinned at him, almost wondering if mother earth had synchronised the encounter so that my parents could see how happy Mr Agent My Man made me.

"Thank you," I said, cupping his cheek as he bent to plant a wet kiss on my forehead.

Turning back to my parents, who shared another look, I smiled. "I will make my own choices."

Gerard frowned as he looked at them, his eyes widening. Grabbing his arm, I squeezed it, silencing him. There were no actual words confirming what I'd meant, but my parents knew what would happen if I chose Gerard. I would lose my link to the ley line, and my inheritance to the Essex witch blood line. And, I would be all the happier, because I'd be with the man I loved.

9

"You're walking well," Justina said as I hobbled along next to her.

Her sarcasm was noted as Gerard opened the door for me. My attention was too riveted by the government building. All old style, the gothic architecture made my stomach flutter. There were some very powerful people in the building that housed Paranormal MI5.

"I feel like a naughty teenager about to be told off by the head teacher," I muttered as we were searched by the human guards on the doors.

Odd to have a weaker person guarding those that were part of a force who protected the paranormal.

Biting my lip, I waited to see if the human found my dagger. My heartbeat was erratic as his hand grazed the pocket on the back of my jacket. I'd placed an invisibility spell on the weapon, just in case of this scenario. Yes, naughty to use my magic to fool the government, but there was no way I was going into a place full of crime executives without some protection. Especially when I was technically an illegal species.

"Okay," the guard said. "Go through."

Limping into the small, but grand, reception, I almost laughed when Gerard tripped over his own feet. He managed to right himself before his arse hit the ground. Throwing me a shut up look, he went over to the receptionist to book us in.

Apparently, Justina had received a call from the government as I lay recovering in the infirmary. They wanted to talk to us about Cameron Fieldman. They would use the Paranormal MI5 building to have our meeting over video call. A part of me was excited to see all the funky things inside a place that ran such a big operation.

My gaze was tracing the ornate painted ceiling, so I didn't notice the agent approach until she spoke.

"Good morning, I'm Gemma Abbott."

Ah, crap. She smiled at each one of us individually. She looked as cool as she had when we'd been on Arthur's seat in Edinburgh. Her brown hair was down today, her flat knee-high boots tied with laces over shiny leather trousers. Her shirt had Book Nerd written on it. Yep, she was a legend. And, my cousin, apparently.

"Please follow me."

Gerard looked at me, his eyebrows raised as she wandered towards the bank of elevators at the back of the room.

"I agree," I whispered. "I would too."

Grabbing my arm, he stopped me as Justina and Kurt continued. "That's not what I was thinking in the slightest. She might bring up the tiny subject of your Essex witch vows."

"Oh. Yeah, hopefully not."

The others were close to the door as it opened. Taking Gerard's hand, I half dragged him to catch up. He let go of me as soon as Gemma stepped into the elevator and spun round. It was probably an excellent idea not to let her know that we were together. Any questions would bring up the fact that Gerard wasn't an Essex witch.

"We're going to the top floor. There are a small team of us here to talk to you, although I'm the only one from paranormal MI5."

As we joined her in the elevator, Gemma tucked her hair behind her ear. Noting the awkward action, I watched as she bashed a button and faced forward, ignoring us.

"This building is impressive," Kurt tried. "I wouldn't mind it for a home."

Glancing at him sideways, Gemma nodded. "Yeah, there's fantastic history here. Did you know that it used to be a library before the government took it over in the war? Such a shame. I bet the book collection was insane."

The doors sprung open before anyone could reply. Striding forward, Gemma didn't wait for us. There was a reception desk directly in front of us. Corridors went off in an oval shape around to the left and the right. Glass panels on the outside were covered with different pictures, each cut off by a line that determined where an office ended. The pictures were random, obviously showing the personality of the agent. Names were above the doors that were set in the centre of each section.

In the middle of the floor, behind the reception desk, there was a clear glass wall that went all the way round to form an oval room.

"That is the best break room I've ever seen," Gerard said, his eyes zoning in on the television and games consoles.

There were sofas, bean bags, and a kitchen area. A painting easel and bookcase were tucked away to one side.

"We often chill in there," Gemma said. "The MI5 know how to treat their agents well."

About to comment to Justina, I paused when the few agents that sat in the break room turned to stare at me. Almost in synchronicity.

"Ignore them," Gemma said to me as we walked. "They're kind of fascinated with your breed."

Really? Top agents in a government agency were interested in me? Well, it was no wonder really. They probably wondered how I could fuck up so often.

My fingers started to tingle as Gemma opened an office door. This one didn't have any pictures, it was an open conference room. The protection spell around it made me itch to use my magic. I'd been holding back, trying to ween myself off. The shakes hadn't set in properly yet, but my body was only just under control. Not that anyone knew.

Breathing slow and deep as we were gestured to sit, side by side, I calmed my nerves. A bank of screens of all sizes were at the end of the room, all of them black. We faced them, our seats behind a big glass desk.

"This is what you call high flying," I said to the others. "Maybe we could kit out the library like this?"

"You have a library?" Gemma asked as she placed a tray of hot and cold drinks on the table in front of us.

Kurt grabbed the beer, laughing at Gerard when he pretended to scowl. "Yes, we have a library with lots of books. You've probably got a library of your own, though? Don't book worms read ten books a day?"

Nodding enthusiastically at first, Gemma quickly recovered, her whole demeanour changing. Her back straightened, her head came up. A calm descended. "Some do, some don't. I don't get time to read as much as I'd like."

The switch from the real Gemma to the agent had been obvious and instant. She was a chameleon, switching who she needed to be in a second. How interesting. I couldn't get a hold of myself enough to be so fluid.

How often did Gerard have to tell me to behave? Or, to switch into agent mode.

The door opened, and a couple of suited men came in. Their briefcases and stern expressions made them look official.

Vampires. Interesting. Working at the Hunted Witch Agency meant that the only criminals we had to contain were the witches. However, paranormal MI5 had to deal with all species. Gemma must have a tough job.

"These are the government officiators. They've come to make sure you're real. They'll sit at the back of the room while you speak to the Prime Minister."

I spat the lemonade I'd been sipping, the liquid spraying over the table. We were speaking to the head of the government?

Without thinking, I swiped my arm to clear the droplets of liquid, cringing when the sleeve of my jacket got wet. Whispering a spell, I smiled when it dried.

Gerard nudged my leg, his face grave. What? I couldn't exactly stay wet, especially if we were going to speak to the prime minister. Although, yes, the small kick of magic had made me feel less jittery.

Looking at her watch, Gemma smiled to herself, quickly clearing her expression when the men at the back had made themselves comfortable.

"You're not allowed to-" Gemma stopped abruptly, looking behind us. "What's the problem?"

A hand grabbed me, hauling me to my feet before I could react. My heart thundered in my head, my breath fast as my stomach flipped. My team were up, their hands raised, ready to use magic if need be.

The vampire who had a hold of me had lifted me off the ground, the heels of my boots an inch from the floor.

Swinging, I thrust out my fist, aiming straight for his jaw. The vampire blocked me with his other hand, a growl coming up his throat as his teeth extended.

"Explain!" Gemma shouted, a blast of light drawing everyone's attention.

Looking over, I didn't know whether to grin or scowl. The bitch was holding a dagger, similar to mine. However, hers was full of white light, pure magic. Mine had never been that intense.

"She has a weapon," the vampire officiator said, somehow getting his hand under the back of my jacket and yanking out my dagger. A slight rip made me wriggle to try and get out of his grip.

"If you've just ruined my jacket, I'm going to magic the hell out of you."

The others had retreated slightly. Ah, yeah, so I wasn't supposed to bring a weapon into the building. I had thought I'd got away with it, but the vampires had heightened senses. He could've probably smelt the silver of the dagger. Bastard.

"Why doesn't it surprise me that you've gone against our rules?" Gemma asked, clicking her fingers at the vampire.

He dropped me, rather unceremoniously, not handing back my dagger when I held my hand out for it.

Gemma approached and took my blade, her eyes widening ever so slightly when the handle hit her palm. "This Essex dagger has been touched by your warlock magic, hasn't it?"

Glaring at her, I tilted my head to the side, pretending not to hear what she'd said. It was none of her business what I did with my dagger.

"You've been allowed to keep this sacred witch heirloom so you can fulfil your destiny. If you keep putting it off, it will be taken back."

"Back?" I barked. "That's mine! I'll do whatever I want with it."

119

"Errr…" Justina said as she stepped forward. "Actually, Devon, I was asked to give it to you."

Huh? What was she talking about? She'd said that she didn't remember where it came from, didn't she? I tried to go back to the time she had given it to me, but too much had happened since then, and a girl like me only had so many memory cells. Most of them were taken up by Mr Gerard Freshwater.

Gemma rested her knuckles on her hips, each dagger still gripped in her hands. "When you applied to the agency, we were told straight away. All Essex witches are monitored from afar by Paranormal MI5. I run the department of-"

"You run a department here?" I blurted, my cheeks warming when she raised her eyebrows. "Sure, you look like you could run a department of lots of-"

"I run it alone. Mainly."

"Your desk friend," I muttered.

The others shuffled on their feet, obviously confused by our conversation. We weren't here to talk about Gemma Abbot. We were here to talk to the government.

A loud ringing echoed around the room. Gemma tucked the daggers into her boot quickly. "Everyone sit!"

Her authority made us jump to do as she bid. Every single one of us. We knew that as soon as she pressed the answer button the face of the prime minister would be looking at us through the screen.

"Are we ready?" Gemma asked.

I was the last one to pull my chair under the desk. Throwing my thumb up, I quickly pulled it back down when the prime minister appeared. The biggest screen on the wall showed her face. I'd never taken any interest in politics, they bored me. I had no interest in people who were above themselves. They thought they knew how to run a country, and yet...

"Gemma, good to see you." The prime minister's voice was silky.

She was the youngest prime minister ever, and a female. There'd been a bit of an uproar when she'd been elected because people didn't think she was experienced enough, being that she was in her thirties. However, she'd been in power for three years, and a lot of good stuff had come from her time in office. Apparently. That's what Justina had told me on the way to the meeting.

"Prime Minister," Gemma said, nodding.

"Ah, Justina, good to speak to you again."

My boss waved, a big smile on her face. Wow, seemed the pair had a friendly relationship after all. Who knew?

"And, of course, Kurt. You're looking good considering you only had surgery last week."

Was Kurt blushing? Did he like our PM? Wow, I'd never seen him react quite so understated.

"I'm an amazing healer," he said in a strong voice. "If you ever need healing, I'm your man. Personal service and everything."

I'd underestimated him, yet again. Gerard glanced at me, a small smile on his lips. I grinned back, happy to be sitting by his side.

"And, this must be Devon and Gerard. I've heard a lot about you. When Justina told me that she would be expanding her immediate team to add another pair of agents, I was apprehensive. She's been so on point working with Kurt, I wondered if you would distract their efforts. Turns out I was wrong."

My legs started to shake as she looked at Gerard. He inclined his head, his expression warm but cool. If that was even possible.

"It's been an honour to serve with Justina and Kurt... and Devon, of course."

Did he just add me on to the end? Rather than putting me first? I was his partner! He should be-

"And, you, Devon. I've heard all about you." The corner of her lip quirked into her cheek.

My anxiety evaporated as I felt the full force of her energy on me. She was human, no denying. And, yet, she had a warmth about her that most politicians didn't.

"Thank you," I muttered.

Thank you? *What the fuck, Devon?* The PM was clearly not complimenting me. Why had I just-?

"Let's get on with business."

Her dismissal was a good thing. I had made a right prat out of myself. The sooner I was out of the building, the better.

"Okay, on the agenda today," Gemma started.

"Forget the agenda, I've just had a phone call from an associate who has been to see Cameron Fieldman in prison." The PM looked down at her notes.

Gemma had flipped her off as soon as she'd looked away from the screen. I covered my mouth, quite sure that the witch would get bollocked if she was caught putting her middle finger up at the PM of the UK.

123

"Cameron is under our jurisdiction," Justina said. "Why is your associate visiting him?"

Humans didn't usually mess with underworld protocols. It made life a lot harder for both sides. The PM technically had jurisdiction anywhere, so Justina probably shouldn't have said that. I would've crapped my pants if the PM was staring at me the way she was my boss.

"He reached out to us, asked to cut a deal for his release."

"He what?" Justina exclaimed. "And, you listened?"

The PM made eye contact with Justina, her strong sense of self overriding any desire to placate the leader of a top witch agency. It wasn't a self-importance thing, it was diplomacy. Ah, now I knew where Justina got her influence from.

"No, we didn't, but we might. He claims that he can get Mackenzie Bruce and Candy Fieldman to confess. He says that he wants to help us solve the case so the humans stop getting killed. There were two more last night. These drugs are still being pushed by our suspects. And, you've not caught them."

Cameron Fieldman had manipulated the government by using our weakness. No, we hadn't caught the pair, but we would. Soon.

"We're working on a couple of leads. We..." Justina stopped talking when Kurt put a hand on her arm.

"Give us another week. If we've not caught them by then, you do what you need to."

The PM considered Kurt's proposal, her gaze distant as she thought. "Okay," she said eventually. "You have one week. If you've not reported back to me with a positive case closed by then, I'm taking over."

The screen went blank. Boy, that was intense. The whole room pulsed as silence filled it.

"The human government taking over an underworld case?" I said to no one in particular.

Movement behind me made me look over my shoulder, ready to fight if I had to. Instead, the vampires were packing up their things, ready to leave.

Gemma stayed quiet until they'd left the room, not bothering to say a word to any of us on their way out.

"You need to wrap up this case. If she takes over, the future of the agency will be questioned. I'm baffled as to why she's so interested in this case. She never..." She shook her head as she trailed off.

Smacking the table, Gerard made us jump. "The Scottish government. They've been influenced by Cameron for many years. Maybe they're putting pressure on the PM."

Kurt wagged his finger. "Yes, you might be onto something there."

"Shit," Justina said quietly. "That means we've got to get Mackenzie and Candy before the week is up."

Gemma came over as we got up from our seats, each one of us in a bit of a daze. The outcome of the meeting had been completely different to what we were expecting. We all knew the consequences if we weren't able to do our job. And, it was scary as fuck.

"If you don't catch them..." Gemma handed me my dagger as we made our way to the door. She looked worried for us, which wasn't good. "...you'll lose your jobs completely."

10

"I haven't worked out since this morning," I said to Mr Sexy but Broody as we walked through the park.

It was late in the day, the sun just going down. There were several humans dotted around, enjoying the last moments of warmth before the night air set in.

"Are you feeling antsy?"

My feet were bouncing slightly. My magic had been under control, no outbursts, no constant little spells. I'd almost been completely clean.

"We've got an hour until we meet Maxwell. Maybe I could jog for a bit."

Grabbing his chest, Gerard feigned shock. "Jog? You?"

Smacking his arm, I laughed when he knocked it back. He chuckled, his hand coming out to catch mine when I went to try again.

"Come on then," he said, bouncing backwards. "Let's do some combat training."

My insides warmed at the suggestive energy that suddenly vibrated through me. There were much better work outs than a fight, but being in the middle of a park, on the way to meet a semi enemy, it would be better to keep my clothes on.

Gerard was getting into the mood, hopping from one foot to the other. His arms were raised, guarding his face. He looked so bloody sexy.

Rushing for him, I threw my fist towards his head. As he went to block, I used my left arm to plant a punch into his side. He grunted, laughing to himself as he came forward. Trapping both my wrists, he turned me so that they were behind my back. The movement was so quick, I couldn't wriggle free.

"See," he breathed as he bent to speak into my ear, "too slow."

The rush of air that filtered down my neck made me shiver. No, I couldn't let him weaken me with his sexy ways.

My leg kicked backwards, colliding with his knee. It started to buckle, but Gerard jumped back, letting me go in the process. Swinging around, I huffed out my breath as my leg flew in a circle, aiming at his head. The tip of my boot missed his skull by one inch. He was lucky.

"You're getting much better," he said as he came forward, his bigger frame towering above me.

Closing my eyes, I resisted the urge to draw magic into me. I had to beat it. I…

"Are you okay?" Gerard's words were whispered, his heat permeating me from where he stood close.

Opening my eyes, I nodded. "Yes, I'm okay, but once the warlock link has gone, I'm going to ask Kurt to help me with that spell to disassociate magic with feeling good."

Cupping my cheek, Gerard bent to kiss my nose. "If you feel that you need it, I think it's a good idea."

Smiling gently, I went to reach up to grab the back of his neck and pull him down for a proper cheeky kiss. His hand caught my wrist, squeezing gently. "I don't think our session is done."

My other arm was already raised by his side, waiting to plough into the hard muscle there. Grunting, I pushed him with my body weight, whipping his gun out of his jacket pocket as he fumbled to catch me.

Laughing, I skipped out of his reach, waving his weapon in the air. A scowl crossed his features before he lunged. Yelping as he collided with my legs, I fell backwards, my butt landing heavy on the ground.

"She's got a gun!" someone shouted from nearby.

Oh shit. I had been careless. Humans might have guessed that we were play fighting before, but brandishing the weapon had been a mistake.

Gerard froze, his body heavy on mine as the woman started to scream. I pushed his shoulders, trying to get him off so we could try to control the situation.

"Do something!" I said as he finally launched to his feet.

Whispering a spell, he calmed the woman who was standing about fifty yards away, waving her hands in the air. She instantly stopped, her mouth going slack.

"We need to get out of here," I muttered.

There were several people approaching. Humans had an innate stupidity mode. They ran towards trouble often, thinking they could be the hero. Every now and then, they succeeded. Rarely when it came to the paranormal though.

Shoving the gun at Gerard, I turned when he took it. "Let's go."

Running was the only option. There were too many of them. If we flashed away, they would report it to the police. If that happened, they would then tell the government, who would give us a warning. We weren't supposed to allow humans to see what we were. If we did, there were harsh consequences.

"I got a bit carried away." I huffed as we were chased across the park.

Yes, more humans were joining in. You had to give it to them, they were stupidly brave sometimes.

"Let's just get to Maxwell's shop."

My heart fluttered in my chest as it pumped the blood around my body. My fitness had improved, especially in the last week, but the thought of going to the place where my life had changed forever gave me chills.

The entrance to the park yawned ahead of us. Once through, we could hide behind the hedge and disappear. Adrenaline raced through my veins, the excitement of the chase reminding me why I was an agent. Not because I'd been careless, but because I wanted to help others. I needed to use my power for good, not for self-gratification.

"You're keeping up with me," Gerard panted. "Your training is obviously going well."

My little legs protested, but I pushed on, propelling through the open entrance and instantly turning right. Gerard was beside me, his long legs skidding to a halt as we ducked behind a tree. Taking my hand, he flashed us to Maxwell's shop.

The road was busy, the rush hour never dying down in London. The shop front was dark, the lights already off. The wonderful world of magic was hidden inside. A trinket shop of pretend magical items for the humans. A real life haven for the warlocks.

Pushing the door, I smiled when it clicked, unlocking for us. My feet stumbled as it swung open too suddenly. Righting myself as Gerard came in behind me, I froze when the door slammed shut.

In front of us stood three warlocks. I didn't recognise them, but their stance was solid. The threat was evident in the balls of magic they each held.

Really? Maxwell had set me up? Looking past them, I spotted the leader behind his counter. Ropes were tied around his generous frame, pinning his arms behind him. A piece of duct tape covered his mouth, silencing him.

"What's going on here?" Gerard asked the three men in front of us.

They were equal of height, but their skin colour ranged from dark to light. Each one stared at me, their eyes full of heaviness. What were they doing? Why would they go against their leader?

The soles of my feet warmed as magic pushed its way up from the ground. It was as if it knew when I might need it. An instinctual thing that existed as the bond between me and the earth had deepened.

"We're taking control of this situation. Other warlocks have tried and failed before us. We won't let that happen."

Whispering a spell, I used a small part of my magic to rip the tape from Maxwell's mouth. He exclaimed in pain as the tape hung from the side of his face.

"You could've done that a little slower," Maxwell muttered, glaring at me.

Tempted to put the thing back on, I glared back. "Way to say thank you."

133

"Shut up!" one of the men almost shouted. "We're in control here, not you."

Scratching my head, I used my other hand to take my dagger out. A good old fashioned magic fight wasn't high on my list of priorities, especially as I was trying my hardest to not use my magic.

"Yeah, yeah, you want to make sure you've got me when the solstice comes so you can steal the link. I've heard it all before."

One of the men grunted as he threw his ball of magic towards me. I ducked low, my knees hitting the ground as my crouch helped me to dodge the light yellow ball.

Gerard's gun fired in the air, drawing the attention of the men. They went still, their gazes glued to Mr Trigger Happy.

"You do realise that if you kill Devon, the link will go with her?" His husky voice was harsh as he kept one eye on them and the other on me as I rose to a stand.

Their expressions were hard as they stared at the gun. It was aimed at the middle one, moving to the others if they dared to even flinch.

"No," I said quietly, looking at each of them. "They want me dead."

Their stares grew harder, the truth in their expression. A small part of my heart sunk as

I realised why. I'd wished for it in the past. Freedom. Impure magic was addictive. It drove people to do things they would never usually do. For a warlock to remain good in a place where evil called to them... it was bloody hard work. Their nature was born from the few who had broken away from the witches all those years ago. They'd changed the course of fate when they'd decided to let the power of magic overrule their good nature. The purity of witch magic had been tainted, which meant they had been too. When the magic broke from the ley lines, forming its own source, it had begged to be used by the warlocks. It was powerful, and yet, almost uncontrollable.

"You don't want the warlock magic to exist anymore," Maxwell said. "Why?"

He wouldn't understand it in quite the same way. I'd felt witch magic. The pure essence was glorious. The man in front of me wouldn't have ever felt it, but in recent times, the addiction I'd had to magic showed me how it could turn a life upside down. If a warlock lost control, his family would be in danger. His wife was always a human. They couldn't have female warlock babies. I was the only one. But, I wasn't a full warlock, only part.

"Nathan lost his baby boy last night," one of them said. "His wife ran away with him. She left a note to say that she'd had enough of him using his magic. She wants to be free of the life he's decided to lead."

The man in the middle scowled at the one who had spoken. "Stay quiet!"

"I understand." My words elicited expressions of disbelief as I held up my dagger, showing that it was loose in my hand. "Hear me out."

"No," the middle one said. "We came here to kill you."

"That's not going to happen." Gerard was calm, his voice level.

The gun was ready to stop them from doing anything stupid. The two who still held magic in their palms moved. The gun went off as I spun out of the way. The balls slammed into a display of Harry Potter merchandise. Items scattered on the floor as the men made a run for it.

One of them clutched his shoulder as he dove towards the back of the shop. Gerard was after them, shouting at me to capture the one who went for the front door.

"STOP!" I screamed.

A rush of magic flew out from me in a circle. It was dark blue mixed with white.

Pure and impure combining together. It smacked into everything in the room, including all three men, Gerard and Maxwell.

The ones who were standing crashed to the ground. One collided with the bottom of Maxwell's counter, another slumped to the floor. The last one flew into the front door, the wire mesh the only thing stopping him from smashing the glass.

I gasped as Gerard bounced into the wall near the back exit, instantly sinking to the ground. Maxwell rocked backwards off his seat, hitting the wall behind him.

Covering my ears at the sound of destruction, I sucked the magic back, falling to my knees when it zipped into me and drained out of my feet.

Toys and trinkets, spells and wands, fell to the ground, every single one knocked off its shelf. My gaze was on Gerard as he cradled his elbow. He slowly sat up, instantly searching for me.

"Are you okay?" he asked.

Nodding, I tried to get to my feet. I couldn't. My legs were like jelly, my arms shaking so badly, I couldn't lift them from where they hung beside me. A sob escaped as I stared at the mess I'd made.

"Maxwell?" I called, my voice so broken, I could barely hear myself.

"I'm alright!" he called from behind the counter.

Two of the men were already crawling to a sit. The third was knocked out cold by the front door. What had happened? One moment, I'd been ready to help Gerard stop the men so we could take them into custody, the next, I'd destroyed the whole place.

"How are you not dead?" I said, not really aiming my question to anyone specific.

"See?" the one who had been shot said. "That's why we don't want warlock magic to exist."

"Bloody hell!" Maxwell exclaimed as his head appeared above the counter. "You blew my binds off, woman." His hair was sticking up, his eyes wide. "You'd be good in a bondage bedroom!"

Huh? I'd just blown the place apart and Maxwell was thinking of bondage? What? I mean... now that he mentioned it, maybe Gerard would be into that. A small smile tugged at my lips when he slapped the countertop. "You do know what just happened, don't you?"

Frowning, I shook my head. They should've died. The man beside the door was starting to rouse, his groan a sign of concussion as he clasped his head. He was also alive. The amount of magic that had come from me would've usually killed any living creature.

"Your pure magic," Gerard said, getting up and picking his way over the debris. "The connection to witch and warlock magic activated at the same time. It mixed the magic, which meant the pure magic saved us."

"Jeez, no wonder the warlocks are desperate to get their hands on you," one of the men said.

My skin grew hot as my insides bubbled. "Don't you see?" I snapped. "It's a fucking nightmare being connected to the warlock magic. You think your dangerous now? Look at what almost just happened? I could've killed my..." My throat closed as Gerard dropped in front of me, placing his hands on either side of my face.

"Your kin?" Maxwell said.

My focus had been on Gerard, but he was right. These people were a part of me. I was one of them. To a degree, anyway.

"Yes."

Stroking Gerard's face, I quickly kissed his lips before shoving to my feet. A burst of

139

emotion came over me. This place had always reminded me of Isaac. Of my time training as a warlock.

Maxwell came around the counter, trying to straighten his smart purple suit. There was no point, it was extremely dishevelled.

Going over, I jumped up and threw my arms around him. Tears ran down my cheeks as he put his arms around me, holding me high and squeezing me tightly.

"Devon, you've rejected us as much as you feel we've rejected you."

He was right. Having my father around had reminded me who I was. My mind had been so full of witch business, I'd almost shoved my warlock side away. When I was a teen, I'd been more warlock than witch. Yet, since I'd met Gerard and found out about the ley line, I'd been dismissive of those who were my kin, my species.

"You were going to lead us at one point," one of the men said when Maxwell put me down.

Wiping my face with my sleeve, I chuckled. "Can you imagine me being better than him?"

The men were staring from the floor, their muscles relaxing. We wouldn't persecute them, although Maxwell could make his own choice about what he wanted to do with them.

"I've been lax," he said, stroking my hair before he looked at Gerard. "With my coven."

My man nodded. He knew what Maxwell was saying. He would deal with his men in his way. He didn't want the agency to get involved.

"I can imagine that Devon has been on your mind a lot since Isaac Senior died." Gerard looked toward the front door.

I instantly knew what he was thinking. Going over to him, I took his hand before he could leave us. "This isn't just warlock business. I need you."

Our gazes locked and my belly flip flopped. "You've never needed me," he whispered.

The others groaned as they got up. Maxwell spoke to them about why I was there, explaining how the solstice ritual would work. He was giving them a lot of information considering they wanted the magic gone.

"I do need you," I said to Gerard. "Always."

His beautiful face watched me as I studied his. A line of blood trailed from a small gash on his forehead. His green eyes were bright as his tongue flicked out to wet his dry lips.

"I love you," he said.

141

"I love you too," I whispered, grinning at him.

"Okay," Maxwell interrupted. "I'm not breaking up the love because I'm jealous." He winked at Gerard as we moved to join him. "It's because we need to sort this. We've literally got two days to finalise plans."

Yes, the solstice. The ritual. My mind was split between Mackenzie and Candy, the government, Mr Lover, and now, my affinity with the warlocks. One that I promised to myself I would never forget again.

Maxwell put his hand on one of the men's shoulders. "These warlocks are decent men. I've fallen behind on Isaac's programme that helps us to keep our magic under control. From tomorrow, I'll have those weekly classes up and running again. Please, will you join me?"

Glancing at one another, the men decided something before agreeing. My father had been the truthful heir to the warlock leadership, but he'd given that up when he'd married my mother. I had then inherited it from him, but the responsibility had been too much.

"I have a suggestion, although I'd need to speak to my father first," I said, excitement making me hop on my feet. "My father used to work as the rehab counsellor. Maybe he could come to work for you again?"

Maxwell's gaze softened as it was drawn to where Gerard and I held hands. "That sounds like a wonderful idea. It would be great to have his expertise."

Trying not to cry again, I looked at Gerard. His face was serious. It was time to get on with business.

"Okay," I said, coughing to clear my throat. "Let's decide how we're going to do this."

The men were allowed to stay. Maxwell wanted them to trust him, so he was appointing them as part of the link team. Each one of them agreed to take a binding oath to keep the secret of the whereabouts of the link. My brain protested, my heart thought it was a good idea. Whatever I felt wasn't important, it was Maxwell's decision.

"I want another tree. An ancient one that has protection against the humans trying to cut it down. It has to be in London. As you know, the London coven are the protectors of the tree because of the heart chakra." Maxwell rubbed his stomach. The familiar gesture made me smile.

"What?" Gerard asked, clearly unaware of warlock history.

143

Maxwell tilted his head to look at him. "Don't worry, pretty boy, I'm sure lover girl can give you a history lesson one day. You should know what you're marrying into. Her family is half warlock."

"Wonder what your kids will be," one of the men said, laughing when we stared at him. "Sorry, none of my business."

For once in my life, I didn't feel judgement around the warlocks. It was a refreshing emotion that made me smile broadly. My cheeks ached as I turned to look at Gerard. He was grinning too, his cheeks slightly pink as they all watched us.

"Either way," he said. "They'll be kickass... and I'll be the fun parent."

Choking, I struggled not to laugh hysterically. "You? The fun one? Okay, Mr Growly-only-happy-because-of-me, we'll see about that."

"Young love," Maxwell said, looking positively green around the gills. "It's sickening."

The others agreed as Gerard took out his phone. "Okay," he said. "Let's get back to business."

"England is the heart chakra of the earth." Maxwell was talking to Gerard, gesturing for him to pass him his phone. "We need an ancient tree. Sorry," he apologised to Gerard as he snatched his phone. "These bastards took mine so I couldn't tell anyone they'd kidnapped me."

A slight groan came from the three men as one of them took the phone out of his pocket and handed it to Maxwell.

The leader was already searching something on Gerard's phone. He wasn't stupid, he knew that there would be much more on a phone belonging to an agent. He could access several things that a normal phone couldn't. Like secret mapping of ancient parts of the city. Magic ley lines were on a private map, only allowed to be seen by those protecting them. My mother had told me when I was young, but I'd never been able to have access to it. There was no point now either. Once I'd given up the ley line, I'd probably have it erased from my mind somehow.

"Right, here..." Pointing at a spot on the screen, Maxwell looked at Gerard. "This is a very old part of London. There must be a tree that's more than five hundred years old in the vicinity." Turning to me, he added, "If you could check whether there's a ley line nearby, I'd like to ask you to perform a blood spell to protect the tree. I don't ever want to lose the link again."

Me? A blood spell? Was he insane?

"That would surely put Devon in danger?" Gerard took his phone back and used the agency's database to search for a detailed map of the area.

Wagging his finger, Maxwell disagreed. "No, not at all. These men will be the only people who know about the link. I'm also going to ask you to do a memory spell on them so they only remember when I say the secret word."

Each one of them shuffled on their feet. This was their punishment. Maxwell wouldn't do anything to hurt them, but they would be under his control. It was pretty clever really.

"The heart chakra," Gerard muttered to himself as he read something on his phone. "Okay, so the earth has energy centres that correlate with what would be on a human. So, the only way to explain it is to use the same chart as a human. So, there's seven chakras slash energy centres and they're all over the world."

"Uh huh," Maxwell murmured, looking at his own phone. "We need to keep the link here in London because it's close to Glastonbury, which is where it's grounded."

"No wonder Vernon Jupiter was after my dad. He probably believed that the Stonehenge coven had more right to look after it considering it's just up the road."

My words were met with a wall of silence. Oops. Bringing up Vernon was probably not a good idea. He'd had a real problem with the London coven. Luckily, we'd managed to kill the seer who was giving him access to earth. His soul would be rotting in hell right now, if there was such a thing.

"Anyway," Maxwell said. "Tradition is tradition. It's been in the care of the London coven since the warlocks were created, so it's best to keep it that way, wouldn't you agree?"

We all nodded, even Gerard. I was like a naughty schoolgirl who had questioned the headmaster.

"I'll do it," I blurted. "The blood spell. It's the least I can do."

It was true. I'd mucked Maxwell around when I was supposed to be leader. I'd then dragged out the inevitable, not bothering to keep him up to date. Adding to it was the accidental robbery of the warlock link. Something that I was definitely not entitled to. No one was. At least, if I cast a blood spell, which was pretty much frowned upon in the witch community, I'd make up for all that I'd done. Hopefully.

"Here," Gerard said, quietly. "Here's a tree that's been recorded as the oldest in the whole area. It's in a back garden. And... oh, the property is for sale."

"Buying a property in London is extortionate." I took out my phone to join the search. "Surely there's a park nearby."

"What do you say, boys?" Maxwell clenched his fists and screwed up his face in excitement. "Shall we open a warlock rehab clinic?" Looking at me, he tapped the end of my nose. "Your father might like to run it for us, but there's no pressure."

For some reason, emotion flooded me. The men were quick to encourage the idea, their faces lighting up. Having the link so close to a bunch of warlocks might be dangerous, but if the secret was kept until the next leader took over, it would be a win win situation.

"I love that idea," I said, jumping up and down when Maxwell did.

"Me too! Although, we'll need your influence to get that house. Tomorrow."

Ah, yeah, that was a point. Although, we could easily pull an agency creepy style operation to get the spell done before the solstice.

"We can do that." Looking at Gerard, I waited to see what he would say.

At first, he looked apprehensive, but his serious expression slowly lightened up. "I don't see why we couldn't pull a few strings." Looking at me, he raised his eyebrows. "We do need to get going if we're going to get some influence on that though."

Ah. He was talking about our little deal with the government. Not only did we have to get the solstice ritual done, we had to find Mackenzie and Candy within the week. Jeez, if we managed it, I'd make a gold medal for each one of us.

11

"I can't believe we're doing this," I whispered to Kurt as we watched Justina and Gerard climb over the wall.

Kneeling, he offered me a leg up. Okay, so I did need help to get into the back garden that held the tree, but still, it was kinda embarrassing.

"It's fine," he whispered. "We cleared it with Gemma at Paranormal MI5. They'll use their government pass to buy the house on behalf of Maxwell and the warlocks."

As soon as he'd finished speaking, I put my boot in his hands, squeaking when he hauled me up. I almost flew over the top of the wall, only just managing to grab on to the edge. Hanging for a moment, I seriously debated whether I had the arm muscles to lift myself up and over.

"Get on with it!" Kurt hissed. "All I can see is your arse."

That was enough motivation to get me going. Grunting, I engaged my biceps and somehow scrambled my feet up the wall, hooking them over just before my arms gave out.

"Just fall," Gerard called from the other side.

The garden stretched out behind him to a gorgeous detached townhouse. My eyes surveyed the area, almost wishing I'd suggested that Gerard and I buy it. Not that we could afford it on our agent salaries. We'd both need to become Justina in order to have enough. Or, maybe Gerard could sell his body. No, that wasn't a good idea. There was no way I could share.

"Devon!"

Almost rolling over the wall, I let myself fall. It was a bloody good job I trusted my man. If he hadn't caught me smoothly, albeit with a grunt, I would've hurt myself. A lot.

"Elegant," he muttered as he put me down and turned back towards the tree.

"I can be elegant," I whispered. "I'm a lady, don't you know?"

Looking over his shoulder at me, he winked. His bright green eyes were highlighted by the rising sun. A pang of fuzzies made my shoulders rise up in a happy shrug as he turned back to the job at hand.

"Stop fawning over him and get over there. We need your blood." Kurt pointed at Justina who stood beside the tree.

The spell was the same as the one cast on the stone in Scotland. I would use my blood to conjure a protection spell around the tree. No one would be able to break it. Except maybe an Essex witch. It was my DNA that made the spell stronger than most. The ancestry lines of Essex witches were no longer connected by DNA. If they were, we wouldn't have been allowed to marry each other and produce children. However, the ley line always recognised the DNA of a descendent.

My breath hitched as I remembered my decision. I would no longer be a proper Essex witch, although the blood would always run through my veins.

"We're ready," Justina said as I strode up to the tree.

The salt and earth circle was around the tree, the candles spaced out. We had to get the ritual done as quickly as we could. We had a busy day of hunting Mackenzie and Candy ahead of us.

"Okay." Going over to one of the candles, I waited for Kurt to join us. "Let's get this done so I can get on with my life."

Instead of going over to his candle, Kurt went to the tree. Putting his ear against it, he... listened?

"Devon." He waved me over. "You need to use your dagger to slice some of the bark. That way, when we do the unlinking spell on the solstice, we can direct it here."

Moving to stand beside him, I took out my dagger. There was a slight crack in the ancient bark, but I hesitated. Cutting it would be like slicing into its skin.

"Don't get all sentimental on me," my boss said. "You eat meat, you hypocrite."

He had a good point. Regardless, I whispered sorry as I cut a small piece of bark from the tree. Mother earth gave so we could survive, but we were quickly taking over, forgetting to thank her. I'd have to do something to change that somehow.

"Let's go," Gerard said, his voice tight.

It wasn't like him to be anxious about a ritual. He was pretty calm and collected, often miserable, but still...

Tucking his phone away as we took our places, he glanced at me quickly. Something was up. What was it?

Instead of saying anything, I started the chant. The others quickly joined, using their magic more than mine so I could keep control. The buzzing beneath my boots heated the soles of my feet. I ignored it, only allowing a small portion of witch magic to siphon through me to complete the spell.

Once done, Kurt gestured for me to join him next to the tree. My mind was on Gerard. He was shuffling his feet as Kurt took my dagger from me. What was wrong with him?

"Give me your arm." He demanded. "And please consent for me to use your blood for this spell."

Holding my hand out, palm up, I recited the words he'd told me to say. "I, Devon Jinx, of Essex witch ancestry, give my blood to protect this sacred tree. If enemies try to break the spell cast here, they will be exposed."

I had no idea what that meant, but I trusted Mary. She'd asked Justina to find the spell in Helena's grimoire.

Closing my eyes, I cringed.

"I haven't done it yet," Kurt said. "Stop squirming."

Taking my hand, he held it softly, almost caressing, although in a supportive way, not sexy. That would've made it completely weird. Not that this wasn't weird anyway.

"Concentrate," he said.

Clearing my mind, I opened my eyes. Kurt lowered my dagger, quickly moving the blade across my palm. The sting made me grit my teeth. I was a big girl, I could handle a little cut.

Blood seeped out of the wound, making my stomach churn. Okay, maybe I couldn't.

Placing my hand on the tree, Kurt recited the spell clearly. It was in Latin. I didn't recognise the words as he held my palm flat against the bark, only lifting it when he stopped speaking.

"It's done."

About to take my hand away, I frowned when he smiled at me. "Let's just fix this."

Leaning down, he brought his mouth near my palm. "Er. As much as I like you Kurt, I don't think that's very appropriate."

Blowing on it, he laughed when I almost jumped into the tree's branches. Ice lined my palm, sealing the wound.

"How did you do that?" I gasped when he let me go.

He put his arm around my shoulders, having to bend down to do so. "I used one of the spells from your grimoire."

Handing me my dagger, he grinned, clearly proud of his new healing ability. I had to admit, it was pretty impressive.

The others joined us, Gerard scratching the stubble on his chin profusely.

"I haven't got a grimoire," I said, not knowing whether to ask Gerard what was going on.

Justina opened her bag and pulled out Helena's book. "Actually, a fair few of these were written by you. When you were a child. Which means you get to keep it."

"Ah, that's... lovely? I think." I took the book, pausing when Gerard looked like he was about to wet himself. "What's wrong, Mr Impatient Man?"

"I just got a text from Mackenzie. He wants us to meet him. He has information, but he'll only speak to me and Devon if we're alone."

All three of us stared at him. We'd been struggling to find Mackenzie, and he just texts us out of the blue. Something must be up.

"We can't let this opportunity go," Justina murmured as she rubbed her tiny weeny belly bump.

"Let us do it." Giving the grimoire back to Kurt, I went over to Gerard and took his hand. "We can meet them straight away, get the info they want to tell us and be back at the agency building before the sun has completely risen."

Justina and Kurt shared a look. They knew that if we agreed to a meeting, we couldn't just arrest Mackenzie. It would be unethical to lead him in and then jump. We would have to let him go after. Which would hurt. A lot.

"Go," Justina said eventually.

Apparently, the pair had had a whole discussion with their eyes. I hadn't even noticed.

Goosebumps rose on my arms. We would get to see Mackenzie again. The temptation to arrest him would be strong, but I was ready to do my job properly.

"I'll record the conversation," Gerard said. "Sending it back to you in live time. That way, if we need backup, you can join us." Pressing something on his phone, he smiled when it beeped.

Justina took out her tablet, clicking something to connect the two devices. "Where does he want to meet you?"

"At London Bridge train station."

Clicking on an app on her tablet, Justina brought up a map. A small light blinked right where we stood in the garden. She would track Gerard's phone. "We'll only come if there's a problem. Otherwise, we'll leave you to it. He might trust you more because he approached you in Scotland."

"He's also aware that you're in a similar situation as him. Being in love with a different breed is difficult." Kurt was distracted by his phone as he spoke.

Glancing at Gerard, I held back the swear words I wanted to throw at Kurt. He had no idea how insensitive he was being. Yes, Gerard and I had agreed to be together, no matter what. We hadn't however, discussed the fact that I would still be half warlock, even when the link was gone. Which meant there would probably be no children in our future. It wasn't fair on them.

"Let's go," Gerard whispered, taking my hand.

We landed in London Bridge station before I could blink. My eyes were watering ever so slightly, so I pretended I was blinded by the bright lights of the main station. It was quiet, hardly anyone around.

"Gerard," a thick Scottish accent called.

Spinning, we strode straight over to Mackenzie, who was leaning against a wall. Alone.

"How are you doing?" he asked, his hand flicking open his long leather jacket to reveal a gun tucked underneath.

Raising his eyebrows, Gerard stood directly in front of him. I stood just behind to the left. The energy that pulsated from him was anxious. Sweat broke out on my palms as I checked around to make sure there were no other suspicious people.

"What do you want?"

Gerard's demanding question was met with a smile. "Oh, no need to be like that. I'm here to tell you the truth."

"Where's Candy?" I asked.

My dagger was in my pocket, although, I did wonder if I should take it out, just in case. A human walked past, head bent with music playing through his earphones. Maybe it wasn't such a good idea. I did still have my magic if I needed protection.

"She's in hiding. Cameron has a huge bounty on her head." He shuffled on his feet, not quite as confident as he was pretending to be. "And mine, of course."

"Do you blame him?" Gerard snapped. "You're killing people."

Mackenzie shook his head violently. "That's the thing, we're not. You were so quick to believe Cameron Fieldman, you didn't take the time to find the evidence. Tell me, what evidence do you have that proves we did it?"

I kept my stance strong when he moved away from the wall. If he wanted a fight, we would give him one. However, something in my gut made me pause. He was right. We were going on circumstantial evidence.

"Why were you at the club the other night?" Gerard tucked his hands in his pockets.

Ah, he was going for the non-threatening vibe. I wouldn't play to that, not when Mackenzie had a habit of disappearing on us. He was still our top suspect in the drug killings.

"We were trying to stop the drugs from being taken. We spoke to some of the people, asking them to give them over."

My snort was met with a glare. Mackenzie's cheeks were pink, clashing with his red hair. He wasn't someone who I'd ever imagine killing tons of people. Doubt was starting to set in.

"Cameron has set us up. I'm the perfect scapegoat. You caught up with him. He knew that you were on to him pretty quickly, so he used my relationship with Candy to manipulate you."

Frowning, I stepped in front of Gerard, leaving him to check for threats. "Why were you at that factory in Scotland? I killed people because of you. If you weren't guilty, why would you run?"

I was as in his face as I could get, considering I only reached his chest. Yeah, being short sucked when I was trying to intimidate someone much taller than me. Maybe my dagger would be better.

My thought was squashed when Mackenzie's eyes started to water. No fucking way. Was he...? Yeah, he was. He was bloody well crying.

"I was there to try and find evidence, like you were. I ran because I saw your reaction, your judgement. I get how bad it looks. Especially the bomb at Cameron's place."

"Yes," Gerard said through his teeth. "Hardly innocent, are you?"

Mackenzie's head hung forward. "The bomb was linked to Cameron's house, which was empty at the time. If you hadn't have managed to break the link, no one at the building would've been hurt. Cameron's house would've blown up instead. I was trying to get him to save his people. To confess in prison. He doesn't care enough about them. He doesn't care about anyone."

Looking at Gerard, I cleared my throat. Everything he said could add up. We would have to check the evidence, but my gut feeling was leaning towards him telling the truth.

"Check Cameron's house. You'll find the explosive there, sitting in the middle of his living room."

Nodding, I agreed that we would. Justina would probably send another agent to Scotland instantly to see if he was telling the truth.

"Do you have any evidence that Cameron is the one poisoning the drugs? He's been in prison, and yet, the deaths are ongoing." My whole body hummed with energy.

If we had the real culprit in custody already, we'd be laughing. The government could shove their ultimatum up their arse. And, we could celebrate a case closed. I was totally ready for this case to be closed.

"No." He sighed. "We've been trying to find it, which is why we searched the club for the drugs. We're amateurs, we don't know what we're doing. Cameron has a team of people who work for him. They'll be running the mob coven for him, including the drugs."

Tapping the top of my arm, Gerard let me know that he wanted to take over again. Swapping places, we kept our expressions calm as we relaxed slightly. Gerard obviously believed him. Otherwise, he would've accused him. He wasn't one to placate someone when he thought they were lying. He was a good agent like that. He was a truth seeker. Ever since he'd let go of the past, he was much more personable.

"How about we make a deal?" he said.

Tilting his head to the side, Mackenzie watched him, his expression telling him to go on. This would be interesting.

"If you're telling the truth, give us three days to find evidence of Cameron's involvement. Once those three days are up, meet us here again. If you're innocent, you have no reason to hide from us."

Tucking his coat around him, Mackenzie nodded. "Okay, I get what you're doing. If you don't get any evidence on Cameron, you'll use me as a scapegoat."

Keeping his body solid, Gerard looked him in the eye. "No, that's not it at all. We're professionals. If you're telling the truth, we'll find the evidence. If not, we'll want to question you further. We never arrest anyone unless we have very good reason to."

The doubtful look on Mackenzie's face was justified. I was ready to arrest him before I came to the meeting. Not that I would've been allowed, but still, it wouldn't have taken much for me to get him on his arse to slap handcuffs on him. Yep, it would probably need him sitting down for me to be able to reach.

"Fine." Mackenzie offered his hand. "I'll be back here in three days regardless. I trust you to keep your word."

Without any hesitation, Gerard shook on it. He would keep his word. My man was honourable, which made him exciting. Which made me smile to myself. I was so going to jump his bones as soon as we got back to the agency building. Watching him work was making me more and more hot and bothered. Maybe it was the lack of magic. My addiction was making me a little itchy, although I didn't feel as bad as I had before. I was actually looking forward to being rid of all the extra power. Mostly.

"Until then." Mackenzie saluted us as he strode away, his gait fast, his gaze searching the almost empty station.

"Did you get that?" Gerard said as he put his phone next to his ear.

Blocking them out, I watched as Mackenzie went through the door and disappeared into the darkness. If he was right, and Cameron was the one who was poisoning the drugs, it changed the whole case. We had to go back to the drawing board.

"Right," Gerard said, bringing my attention to him. "We'll head straight back."

As he turned to me, I reached out to wrap my fingers in his shirt. He tucked his phone into his pocket, his eyebrows raising as the corner of his lip quirked. "It's been a productive night," he said, his husky voice going deeper as I pulled him towards me.

Keeping eye contact with him, I bit my bottom lip. "It really has."

"You're changing." His jaw clenched as he cupped my face. "The addiction is releasing its hold on you. I've never seen you so…"

"Sexy?" I inquired. "Scatty? Or maybe-"

"Soft."

Soft? I wasn't soft, I was… melting under his gaze. It was all him. Well, and all the

165

lessons I'd had to absorb over the last few months as an agent. Good times, and bad, had shaped me. And, yet, there would be many more to come.

"You're not fighting me on that?" he said, his gaze narrowing.

Trying not to smile, I lowered my gaze. It only landed on his chest, because you know, he was still holding my face. "I don't want to fight you."

His chest rose as he took a deep breath. "Look at me," he whispered.

When our gaze met again, I gasped. He was so beautiful. He had also softened, even more than I had. In fact, he could almost be called Mr Kind Hearted Softy. It wasn't quite as sexy as my previous nicknames though.

"How about yourself?" He rubbed his thumb over my lip.

Suppressing a shiver, I swallowed hard. "What do you mean?"

"Do you want to fight with yourself?"

What was it with emotions flooding me all of a sudden? He was right. I was changing, but I didn't know why.

"No," I whispered. "I don't want to fight myself."

Leaning forward, Gerard kissed me on the forehead, then the nose. When his lips landed on mine, they pressed gently, not intruding, not too sexy. The kiss was sensual, supportive, and extremely loving.

Pulling away, he wiped the tear that had fallen from my eye. My heart was beating hard, my stomach was fluttering, but I kept eye contact, even though I wanted to look away.

"I love you." His voice was quiet, deep.

A shudder made my body hum much more than any magic could. His love was so much better for me. Not that I would rely on him for my happiness. No, I was a twenty first century woman. I needed to find my own happiness. Then we could come together and have all the happiness, all of the time, forever and ever. Okay, it was probably overkill, but still.

"I love you, too."

Our next kiss grew a little heated. Both of our phones buzzed, making us jump. When that happened, it meant Justina was trying to get hold of us. Gerard had only spoken to her a moment ago, was something wrong already?

"Bubble burst," I muttered as we let go of each other.

Gerard was the first to read the message. "Shit!" he exclaimed. "The government let

Cameron out of prison three hours ago. They don't know where he is."

12

Dragging my slippers as I went to the library door, I didn't even bother to knock. Who in their right mind would call a meeting at six in the morning?

"Nice of you to join us," Justina said as she came over and plopped a mug of coffee in my hand. "You're twenty minutes late."

Gerard, looking all awake and shit, winked at me as I lowered myself into my favourite armchair. When I yawned, my mother frowned in my direction. I'd had five hours sleep. It wasn't enough for my little brain. I needed all the help I could get to keep my mind working, including as much sleep as possible.

"I'm..." Glancing at the clock on the wall, I cringed. "...late. Sorry."

Gerard had set the alarm for five forty-five. I'd heard it but hadn't quite been able to force myself to wake up. Once my man had left, claiming that he wouldn't get into trouble for me, Kingsley started squeaking loudly. The little bugger had become my personal alarm clock, driving me insane with the noise. Finally, I had fallen out of bed and given him a biscuit. His cute kiss against my finger made me forgive him instantly.

"We've had a call from the PM. She said that her team put a tracking spell on Cameron, but he must have disabled it straight away." Justina handed me a piece of old parchment paper.

The spell on it wasn't familiar, but the Essex family symbol, or one of them anyway, was drawn in the bottom left hand corner.

"Great," I said, handing it to my mother. "I suppose Gemma Abbot cast the spell for them?"

Tipping her head once, Justina went back to her desk. She pointed at the bank of CCTV screens to her left. "A camera in East London has managed to trace Cameron Fieldman walking towards the docks."

Kurt leant over the desk to pick up a croissant from the tray of sweet breakfast things. My stomach audibly rumbled as soon as my eyes saw it. Justina swallowed hard, her eyes instantly averting. Pregnancy sickness must be awful.

Without uttering a word, Kurt threw me the pastry, laughing when I only just caught it in my fingers. A flashback to the day I had come in for my interview and the cup of tea that almost fell off the table made me smile. So much had happened since then.

"I want Devon and Julia to try and trace Cameron using the spell. Your connections combined might help."

Her unspoken words about my mother helping to support me while I was in the midst of my addiction were loud. Only to me though. Everyone else was staring at the screen where Cameron was walking down the road, checking over his shoulder once.

"See, there?" Justina said, pausing the video. "His eyes widen, which means he's noticed something, or someone, behind him. He then reaches for his phone."

"I wonder if the government had him followed," Kurt said.

Justina put a hand over her mouth, her eyes blinking. I'd been chomping on my pastry, but seeing her almost vomit made my chewing slow down. I couldn't watch her puke up, it would make me do the same.

"Shall we try the spell now? Just so we can see if it will be easy to trace him?"

She waved me away, turning from us as she fought to control the morning sickness. My mother got to her feet, bringing the spell with her as I indicated that she followed me.

"I'm glad you did that," she said as we exited the library and made our way to the small living room.

We kept a big map of London on the table in there. It would help us to try and locate Cameron.

"I just hope Kurt gives her something to stop the sickness," I said, my mind suddenly snapping awake. "Shit, it's the solstice tonight."

My mother's arm came around my shoulder as we stepped into the living room. I'd been a little distant with her since she'd told me that she'd basically arranged a marriage for me. My skin heated as I tried not to shrug her off.

"You'll be fine. If we focus on Cameron for a few hours, you can then turn your attention to that. It's not until midnight."

Footsteps sounded as my father came in shortly after us. Going over to the table, I placed my hands on the surface to look down at the map. I did not need a family meeting. I needed to wake up and concentrate.

"Right," I said, holding my hand out to my mum. "If we do the spell together, we can hopefully latch on to the remaining trace of energy. I don't know how he's managed to disable it considering how powerful Gemma must be."

Moving to stand beside me, my mother handed me the piece of paper. She looked down at the map, her eyes unable to meet mine.

"I'm sure he's probably just hidden himself. Gemma is very powerful, but together, we can find him." Her voice was quiet, placating.

"Okay," I said, huffing out my breath as my father stood on the other side of the table. "I can tell you want to say something."

"We don't really have time, but we want to apologise for what we did," my father said, waving his hand when my mother went to speak. "No, I'm sorry, Devon. We were wrong to try and intervene in your life. We've seen what our choices have done to you. We thought that we might be able to redeem ourselves if we could somehow help you."

It went silent, our breathing the only sound in the room. My heart was heavy as my father rubbed a hand over his face. I'd never seen him so passionate, so riled up about something.

"It's fine," I said slowly, deliberately. "I forgive you. For everything."

He frowned at me, his eyebrows pulled low over his brown eyes. "Do you mean that?"

Glancing at my mother, I smiled. She was watching me closely, her hands clenched by her sides. Was she worried that I was being flippant? I did have a habit of brushing people off so I didn't have to deal with them.

"I mean it." Taking my mother's hands, I unclenched them. "I love you both very much. It's taken some time to get used to you being here. I've worked with my therapist to let go of the resentment I held for you."

My father came around the desk. Putting one arm around my mum, he did the same to me and drew us both in for a hug. "It makes me very happy to hear that you've forgiven us. We're always going to be here for you. Regardless of what you choose for your life. We'll no longer try to interfere. Just... choose a good man."

I'd been sniffing his fatherly scent, the familiar smell making me close my eyes. At his words, I pulled back. "You don't think Gerard's a good man?"

Putting his hand on my head, he looked down at me. I felt small then, like a child again. His acceptance of the man I loved meant more to me than I had first realised. I was prepared to go it alone, prepared to accept their dislike of my decisions, but deep down, I was like any person. I wanted their support.

"Yes, he's a good man."

A small noise from my mother made me look at her. She waved a hand in front of her face. "It's just... the consequences that worry us, but only because we love you."

Okay, now we were moving on to territory that I wasn't ready to talk about. That conversation would come when the solstice was over and Cameron was either in prison or dead.

"Let's get on with the spell. Justina will be expecting us to return soon."

Both of them hugged me tightly before they let go. My throat suddenly threatened to close, but I quickly pushed the emotions away and clicked into agent mode.

"Right," my mother said, putting the piece of paper on the table between us. "Let's do this."

My father moved to the other side again, ready to tell us if the tracking spell worked when we tried to link back into it.

Taking my mum's hand, I glanced at her to confirm she was ready. She smiled broadly, her energy much lighter than it had been when we first walked into the room.

Reading the spell, I memorised it as quickly as I could before closing my eyes. My mother's fingers tightened on mine as I started the chant. She joined in after the first round. The link that connected me to the ley line was strong as I felt into it, envisioning the pure white magic, ethereal under the surface of the earth. My feet were cool as I tugged some into my body, the feeling intensifying when my mother did the same. We were hooked into the same line, our blood connecting us both.

Heat bubbled under my soles as the warlock magic tried to gain entrance. Refusing it, I almost felt sad that I was using my witch magic more often than not. I loved both sides of me, but the pure magic was a little easier to resist.

The chanting echoed around the room as it grew louder. The room grew warm as our magic zoned in on the location of Cameron

Fieldman's DNA. Justina had made sure to take a sample from our database.

"It's done," my father said.

We both finished the last part of the spell before we opened our eyes. A small smile passed between us before we looked down at the map. It was an honour to link into the ley line with my mother. It might even be the last time.

Blinking, I cleared the thought quickly. I couldn't think about what I would miss if I gave up my connection to the ley line, I had to think about what I would miss if I didn't. Gerard far outweighed magic. My mother would always be my mother, regardless of what journey I chose.

Leaning forward, I spotted where a bright red splodge had appeared on the map. It wasn't blood. In fact, I had no idea what it was. Still, it was showing a hotel underneath it. That was handy.

"He's in South London," I said, looking up when Justina, Kurt and Gerard came into the room. "Staying in a hotel by the looks of it."

"Good work," Justina said, marching over and examining the map. "Julia, Kevin, if you could watch the map, we'll go and stake him out."

"It's moving," my mum said, pointing at the red mark.

She was right, it was tracking down the road beside the hotel. We had to get there fast, before we lost him. There was a risk that he realised that the tracking spell had been reactivated.

"Let's go," Justina said, getting out her gun. "Stay behind me. We want to see where he goes, not capture him straight away. I'm betting he'll check up on his enterprise. He has no idea that we even know that he's out. The government said that they promised him that they wouldn't tell us so he could collect the evidence needed to get Mackenzie."

"Are they fucking idiots?" Gerard spat, his face screwed up.

Laughing, I got my dagger out as I rounded the table and fell in line with my colleagues. The human government really didn't know what they were doing when it came to the paranormal underworld. Why were they getting involved?

"They are fucking idiots," Kurt said, nodding at my parents as he zipped up his leather jacket. "Let's go and get this motherfucker."

Before I could say goodbye, Gerard grabbed my hand and did a relocation spell.

We landed in the street we'd just seen on the map. Spinning as I searched the people who rushed down the road, I kept my dagger tight in my grip, just in case. Cameron's back was retreating around the corner, his dark navy suit moving perfectly with his frame.

"There!" I said to the others as they also searched. "He just turned left."

We ran, dodging those who were in our way. Being conspicuous wasn't great, but we didn't have time to tip toe. We were going to catch the bastard out, otherwise I would resign myself.

As we rounded the corner, his back strode down the walkway, moving through the rushing throng of people. They were all on their way to work. Rush hour wasn't the best time to be tracking someone.

"Shit," Justina said when he disappeared. "He's gone. Julia," she barked into her phone. "Which way did he go?"

We let Justina take the lead as my mother told her which direction he had taken. A couple of humans frowned at us, muttering under their breath when we shoved our way past. It was London, we were British, what did they expect?

Except, they were probably curious as to why we were moving in unison, our sexy outfits telling a story they had no idea about. It was fun being an agent. Sometimes.

My dagger was tucked close to me, as were the others' weapons. We didn't want to cause panic in the street. It would look bad. Not only on the agency, but on the underworld. The government were precious as it was. We didn't need to give them any excuses to enforce even stricter laws.

"Down this way," Justina said quietly, making us wait behind her as she checked around the corner of the end of the street.

Obviously it was clear because she waved us forward. Overtaking, I marched, my gaze glued to our enemy's back. He had to be leading us somewhere. If he wasn't, I was sweating for nothing.

He was heading into an industrial area. Factories and office blocks meant that the atmosphere was different. Less people, more fumes. The same amount of cars. London never slept.

"Where is he going?" I whispered to Gerard as we waited, trying to stay hidden by the few people around.

Just as he looked over his shoulder, we ducked behind a phone box. I almost tripped, my boots slipping out from under me. Gerard's arm caught me around the waist, hauling me upright again. He was my hero.

"He just changed course," Justina said, getting the info from my mother.

We pushed on, our footsteps parallel to each other. Well, almost. Mine were double the others, but I was still beside them.

Reaching a side alley, Justina poked her head around. We waited for her command. My insides shivered at the idea of catching Cameron out. Surely, he was leading us to evidence. If not, there was a good chance I would explode.

"Okay." Justina gestured for us to follow her.

All four of us were on edge, our weapons ready, our nerves shaking. Or, at least mine were, anyway.

"He's gone into that building," Justina whispered as she pointed to a grimy door.

The back entrance was unremarkable, almost invisible. Tons of rubbish lined the ground, a faint waft of it filling the air.

About to thrust myself down the alley, I halted when Justina stuck out her arm to stop me. I backtracked as Kurt pulled me onto the main street.

"You're going to get on higher ground and watch the building. When Cameron comes out, we'll storm it at the same time as grabbing him." Justina pointed down the road. "Devon, Gerard, go and see if there's an alleyway that connects further down."

Nodding, we marched away, careful to remain casual. Gerard took my hand with his free one, smiling down at me when I blushed. It was unlike us to walk along, holding hands, just like a normal couple.

"If this gets nasty, you need to get yourself out. You have to be in Scotland tonight to do the ritual."

My heart sped up. He was right. If anything went wrong, I could be in danger of not getting the warlock link removed. Why hadn't I thought about that?

"Maybe it wasn't such a good idea to come," I murmured, letting Gerard lead me down another alley.

He pointed at a ladder that ran up the side of the building. I went before him, trying not to giggle when I paused to get a better grip and he head-butted my arse.

"This is hardly the time, Mr Eager Agent," I said, looking down.

His teeth were gritted as he glowered at me. "Keep going, I'm not exactly a fan of heights."

About to carry on, I paused when our phones beeped. That would be Justina. There was no point in waiting until I'd climbed to the top. Just in case we needed to go down again.

"Reverse," Gerard said before I could get my phone out. "Justina said he's left already. They didn't have time to grab him."

Fiddling with my jacket, I let go of one of the rungs. My balance was precarious as I went to lower my boot. My fingers slipped as the tip of my boot missed the edge of the rung. I started to fall, the wind pushing my hair so it whipped around my face. Gerard shouted a spell, freezing me in mid-air. My back was only inches from the ground. I hadn't been too high, but the hard landing would've hurt.

"Thanks, babe," I said as Gerard took my arm, released the spell and dragged me to my feet.

Indicating that we should go, he jogged away. I went with him, the shakes that moved through me slowing me down. That had been a close call.

Coming back into the street, we checked that no one was watching. Moving closer to the alley where we'd left the others, we both thrust down it. My nerves were rattling, which meant something was going to happen. I was already on edge from the impending ritual, but catching Cameron out was high on my needs list.

Justina put a finger to her lip as we approached. She held her gun beside her face as she approached the door. Kurt followed, his own weapon drawn. They all used guns. I was the only one with a dagger. Not that I minded, my dagger was precious to me. And, I was a kickass aim with it. A gun? Not so much.

Turning to us, Justina counted down with three of her fingers. When the last one was tucked into her palm, she aimed the gun at the door lock and shot. The loud noise made me cover my ears. Before I could blink, the door was pulled open, and the others had gone through.

Keeping close to Gerard, I smiled at the sound of shouting coming from a room that was at the end of a corridor. The place was grim and smelt of magic. If that was even possible. I couldn't describe what the smell was as we thundered down the corridor and burst into the big room.

"Freeze!" Justina shouted as five witches were revealed.

All men, they were running out from behind long tables. The stench of unwashed bodies reached me, almost making me wretch.

The room was dim with only a few dirty windows and old light bulbs illuminating the place.

"Stop!" Kurt aimed his gun at the ceiling and shot.

The men ignored him, most of them diving for a door at the back of the room. Two of them came towards us, their growls threatening.

"You shouldn't have come here," one said. Extending his arm, he shouted a spell. "*Incendia!*"

Fire ignited around us, the flames heating our bodies. I glanced at the others, my conscience torn. Not one of them looked at me. Instead, they were looking for a way around. Putting fire out was hard, not many witches could do it. Except me. If I used all my power, I could do it.

"I can't get through," Kurt called as he checked the line of fire that went from one end of the room to the other.

"Shit," I muttered, catching sight of the witches as they ran for the end of the room.

We needed to arrest at least one of them to persuade them to testify against Cameron.

Holding out my hand, I started the reversal spell. Gerard grabbed my elbow, knocking my arm down. "Don't," he said. "Your addiction."

"This will be the last time. I can't let them get away."

His face screwed up, but he pointed at the fire. "Do what you need to do."

Closing my eyes, I restarted the chant. My words were quiet as witch magic swirled up my legs and into me. Holding the dagger tightly, I drained some of the magic into it for balance. The handle was cool in my palm, a stark contrast to the heat that came with my warlock magic.

"It's wavering," Kurt shouted. "Hurry!"

Pushing my magic into my words, I almost laughed when the heat from the flames evaporated. The others were gone before I could open my eyes. The witches were right near the door, almost fighting each other to get out.

Gritting my teeth, I threw up my arm and cast a barrier spell on the door. The rush of wind that flew from me travelled through the room, moving Justina's loose hair as she ran down the middle aisle of the tables.

"We fight!" I heard one of the witches say.

Most turned towards us. I strode down another aisle, slightly behind the other three. Warlock magic burnt my feet as it tried to gain entrance. My step faltered when I let it enter me. The heat seared my bones, making me gasp. It had been a while since I'd allowed so much energy into my body.

Grabbing the side of a table, I steadied myself as the witches formed a line. Each placed a hand on the others shoulder to connect their magic. Every one of them looked in my direction.

"You're that half-breed!" another of them shouted.

"We need to end her!"

End? What a funny word. Nothing really ended. Something new was always put in place. If I died, if anyone died, our bodies went back to mother earth, and our spirit went back to the main energy source.

My hair was flying as I righted myself. Too much magic swirled within me, but I wasn't about to go down. These people were evil. They knew exactly what they were doing. The bottles of drugs were laid out all around me, mixing bowls beside them. Huge vats of poison were near where the culprits stood.

"Devon," Gerard called. "Be careful!"

Kurt and Gerard moved to get closer to the men, but they were stopped by a barrier spell. They both looked at me, but I was too interested in the poison. How would they like it if I injected them with it?

A Gunshot fired. At first, I thought it was my people, but the sound of the bullet whistling past my ear made me cringe. Bastards. I would make them pay.

A whisper of words created a crack of bone as the man holding the gun suddenly fell to the floor, his weapon skidding across the ground. Yep, I'd broken his wrist. Served him right for firing at me.

"Devon!" Gerard caught my attention as another witch stared above my head.

Looking up, I only just managed to throw myself to the side, my elbow scraping the concrete below me as a chain came crashing down from behind.

Jumping up, I aimed my hand towards the man, almost smiling to myself when his knees buckled and he clasped his head. A little brain haemorrhage would help him sort his priorities.

Someone grabbed me from behind. Swinging my arm, I grunted when Gerard trapped me against him. "You're losing control," he whispered. "Come back to me."

Blinking rapidly, I took a deep breath, almost gasping back to life. Kurt and Justina had managed to break through the barrier spell and were fighting the witches with their bare hands.

"I got a bit lost there," I said as I turned.

Shaking my whole body to rid myself of the hold the magic had on me, I clung to Gerard's hand. He nodded quickly when I ran a hand over my hair, bringing it back into some form of messiness. The wind hadn't helped my lack of style situation.

"Let's go."

Marching away from me, Gerard approached the group who were scuffling with the others. About to join them, I froze when one of them took out a knife and aimed it for Justina's stomach.

"NO!" I screamed, the force of my voice causing everyone to turn towards me.

Lifting my arms, I decided to take matters into my own hands. Justina, Kurt and Gerard backpedalled across the room when I almost sang a spell. The vats of poison started to shake violently. The witches tried to run, but I stepped forward, my hand stopping them with a wall of fire. As they went back to the door and pounded on it, I brought my hands close together and hummed to myself. The link to the warlock magic pulled hard, causing bright green magic to pour from my fingertips to form a ball. Without thinking, I launched the ball at one of the big wooden vats. The magic was so powerful, it smashed against the wood, causing it to explode into a thousand pieces. The liquid flew everywhere, igniting the fire further. Screams echoed around the room, coming from the witches who had been hit with the very thing that they had been working with. If I was correct, it would be high potency, which meant they would be burnt if it splashed onto their skin.

"Devon," Justina said, grabbing my arm. "Put the fire out. If you don't, we won't have any evidence."

Taking a deep breath, I whispered a spell that made the fire vanish. On the other side of it, the witches were on the ground. A couple were motionless, their bodies steaming from the burns. The rest were cradling different parts of their bodies, their gazes glaring at me.

"You're all arrested for the murder of several witches and humans throughout the country. You do not need to say anything..."

I tuned Kurt out as he and Gerard handcuffed the witches who were still alive.

Justina put a hand on my shoulder, breaking me out of a trance. "Are you okay?"

My whole body shook as the excess magic drained away. Tears mixed with sweat as my knees buckled, and I hit the ground. Justina was there, her hands checking me over.

"It took control," I said, barely able to talk.

"I know." Her words were strong as she placed her arms around me. "It's okay. Let's go home."

Before I could reply, we landed in the living room of the agency. My mother and father were sitting on the sofa, arm in arm. When they saw us, they rushed over.

"Look after her. We need to clean up."

Justina was gone again, leaving the cool air to envelope me. My parents replaced her, my father digging his arms under my legs to lift me. Taking me to the sofa, he laid me down. My mother tucked a blanket around me. I was shivering so hard, my jaw rattled.

"What happened?" my father asked.

"The magic took hold." My voice was shaky as I inhaled several deep breaths to calm myself. "We have the evidence. We can get Cameron. But..."

"What is it, my love?" My father was sitting beside me, his hands holding mine.

191

Tears streamed down my face as the memory of the power that radiated throughout me in that factory made me want to go to sleep and forget it. I'd never been so powerful, but in that moment, I didn't want any magic. I didn't want to be a witch, or a warlock. I wanted to be Devon Jinx, the girl who covered her pain with snark, the one who loved a man who was deeply troubled and good at singing. The person who wanted to help others, but somehow ended up hurting them.

Taking a deep breath, I looked into my dad's eyes. "Please," I pleaded. "Get this link out of me. Now."

13

"I should come with you," Gerard said, taking my hand as I tied my bootlace.

Smiling, I cupped his cheek. "You need to stay and help the others with the witches. I'll be fine. Mary said it would only take a few minutes at midnight."

Justina had to talk to the PM via Skype. Kurt needed Gerard's help to get the evidence from the factory before it was contaminated. I needed to go and get rid of the warlock link. We all had a job to do.

"It's fine," I said when he hung his head. "My parents are coming with me. So is Maxwell. Bradley's dead, the stones are protected."

His sigh turned into a primal growl as he rose quickly from his feet, pushing me back on the bed as he landed on top of me. I giggled as he went still, looking down into my eyes.

"I want to be there for you in everything," he whispered, his green eyes dull as he leant forward and kissed my forehead gently.

Stroking his stubbled jaw, I stared at him, unable to believe that he was mine. For a long time, I'd remained single, not able to find the right person to support me. To accept me. I'd not been unhappy, I'd been on a journey. And, now, I couldn't imagine life without him. The one thing I'd needed through my growing pains as an agent was the space to be held. He'd managed to stick with me, even though I'd been through hell and back. He was a keeper. A very sexy one at that.

"You are always there for me. I don't think I would be here right now if it wasn't for you."

His lips descended to mine. My fingers stroked the short hair at the back of his head as my skin warmed gloriously.

"Time to go!" my father shouted, banging on my bedroom door.

Kingsley squeaked, reminding us of his presence. Gerard grunted as I gently shoved him, laughing when he pinned my arms above my head.

"I love you, Devon Jinx, no matter how much magic you've got."

"Even if I had none?"

My whispered words made him frown. "Yes, even if by some miracle, you had none. Now, let's get that link out of you so we can get back to our job."

Scrambling off me, Gerard helped me to my feet. One last kiss made me weak at the knees. Kingsley squeaked again, forcing me to detach myself from my man and go to him.

"I won't be long, little guy," I told him as I stroked his head through the bars of his cage.

He nudged me, whimpering when I gave him a biscuit and made my way to the door. Gerard held it open, a grin on his face as he went to grab me. Dodging out of the way, I looked over my shoulder at my best friend. Something wasn't quite right with him. He hadn't eaten his biscuit. He always ate his treats. Instead, he watched me, his tiny little eyes somehow telling me to be careful.

"Come on," my father said, reaching in to the room and dragging me into the hallway.

"We've literally got twenty minutes until midnight."

My mother rushed up to us, taking both our hands as she did. Gerard put a hand on each of their shoulders before we could disappear. "Take care of her."

The last thing I saw before we flashed away was his beautiful face. A worried look had crossed it just before we left, but I knew that he would never be happy with not being with me. Still, it had to be done. He had a job to do. So, did I.

We landed in the middle of the Clava Cairns clearing. Mary stood beside the tall stone, her hand resting gently against it. Maxwell was examining the round burial structure, built of ancient smooth stones nearby.

"Well, good evening," Mary exclaimed as she shuffled over.

Throwing her arms around me, she almost recoiled as my hands patted her back. Slowly disengaging herself, she smiled at me. "I'm sorry, dear, but you're full of magic. It's rather zingy to a non-magical being such as myself."

Hearing voices, Maxwell joined us. "Glad you could come, you've left it a little late."

He looked over to the left, scowling when the three men who had threatened us came closer. "What did I tell you? Stay away from the inner circle. Get back to your posts."

The warlocks rolled their eyes as they reversed, clearly bored.

"How long have you been here?"

"Most of the day," the warlock leader chirped as he rubbed his big stomach. "Nice to see you, Kevin. Did Devon tell you about my proposition?"

My father nodded as he offered his hand. I cringed when Maxwell extended the one he'd just been touching his stomach with. Ew.

"She did, thank you. I'd very much like to work with you at the rehab centre."

Something passed between them. Respect? I sure hoped that was what it was, anyway. I couldn't wait for my father to help the warlocks. It would be good for him to sink his teeth into something meaningful. My mother had been an important part of the agency. She was a witch, which meant she could work with us. However, my father, as much as he'd helped, wasn't actually an official agent. He couldn't be, he was a warlock.

"We haven't got time to talk." Mary took my hand and pulled me towards the main stone.

My parents took their positions either side of me. If, by some miracle, there was a threat, they would be there to protect me. My father had started to use his warlock magic again, albeit very slowly. He had been powerful in his day, apparently. I'd never seen it as a child because they'd predominantly wanted to bring me up a witch.

"So," Mary started. "When the solstice hits at midnight, your mother will recite the spell that she found in the grimoire. It's a relocation spell. Your blood has bound the stone to the tree in London. Once the portal is opened, you'll cut your hand again, placing it on the stone. It will then take the link out of you and redirect it to the tree. The essence from the bark that you cut has been rubbed onto the stone."

Considering Mary wasn't a witch, she knew a lot about the ritual. When we'd first met, she'd not only fawned all over my boyfriend, she'd told me that she wasn't going to get involved in my business. She'd been a huge help. I would repay her someday.

Maxwell moved to stand slightly away from the stones. I trusted that he'd briefed his men. If any of them tried to access the link between the time it was taken from me and put into the stone, we'd have major issues. However, that wasn't my problem. I might be half warlock, but Maxwell had taken the leadership, which meant he'd also taken responsibility.

"I'm sorry this happened," I told him as he watched me. "I do respect you, even if I've not shown it very often."

His face grew softer as he came over and offered his hand. Taking it, I laughed when he brought it to his lips and kissed my knuckles. "Devon Jinx, you've kept me on my toes. You'll always be a part of the London warlock coven. Isaac Senior accepted you as a half breed, and so do I. Now, give us our link back and all will be well."

"Don't I know it," I muttered, taking a deep breath.

"Okay, everyone." Mary shooed Maxwell away as she guided me to stand right next to the stone. "We haven't got long."

My mother was by my side, her eyes glazed with unshed tears. "I'm so proud of you," she whispered when we made eye contact.

"Me too," my father piped up. "Although, you've almost given me a heart attack numerous times recently. Let's just get this done so we can get on with our lives."

Hugging them both spontaneously, I closed my eyes and breathed them in. I finally had my whole family, and it didn't feel dysfunctional anymore.

"Well, isn't this sickly sweet," came a familiar male voice.

Releasing my parents, I turned to face the impossible. "Vernon Jupiter, how the fuck are you here?"

The warlock was standing directly where I'd killed Bradley. His eyes were bright red as he grinned manically, waving at us in greeting. "I managed to connect to Bradley after you killed Helena and sent me back to hell. Thanks for that by the way."

His grimace was satisfying, even if it only lasted a moment.

"You're welcome," I replied.

My hand wrapped around my dagger handle, bringing it out of my pocket. I didn't leave the agency building without it, even if I believed that I wouldn't need it.

The beating of my heart increascd when Vernon took a step forward. What did he want? He would not ruin the ritual. I was

200

sick and tired of people trying to bring me down.

"When you killed Bradley, you opened up a tiny slit from hell. It's okay, it was my energy print, so I was the only one who was able to come through it."

"Oh, well, that's okay, then." I sneered as I stepped in front of my parents.

Maxwell's warlocks started to advance, their intent clear from the balls of multi-coloured magic in their hands.

"I wouldn't, if I were you," Vernon said as he bent his head to look over his shoulder.

Maxwell was poised nearby, his arms raised and ready to fight.

"Vernon, this is our fight." My father drew his attention away from the leader of the warlocks. "Let's go somewhere to sort it out."

Throwing his head back, Vernon let out a high pitched laugh. Ugh. I'd forgotten how creepy he was. Not only was he insane when I killed him, but Helena had brought him back from the dead. He was still dead, but his soul was branded by hell. He was pure evil.

"I don't think so," the previous leader of the Stonehenge warlock coven hissed. "Your lovely daughter has something I want."

My knees bent slightly, my stance strong. Okay, so he wanted a fight. It was only moments away from the solstice, so I had to put him down quickly.

Pointing my dagger to the ground, I crouched further, touching the tip to the dirt. Pure witch energy instantly zapped into the blade causing white flames to lick it before they disappeared.

"Let's play," the spirit warlock shouted.

Spinning, he threw out a steam of black and red magic. It soared through the air, hitting all the warlocks, including Maxwell. They instantly fell to the ground, their bodies convulsing. Shit, that was dangerous. Really dangerous. Evil magic went beyond anything I could handle.

Glancing over my shoulder, I gestured for my dad to protect my mum and Mary. He nodded, dragging them both into the middle of the cairn closest to us. As Vernon faced me, I kept my gaze on him, throwing a protection spell around the cairn to protect my family.

Rushing forward, I extended my dagger arm, throwing the magic out. It flew forward, grazing Vernon's arm as he ducked to the side. My momentum kept me going as he howled, clasping the area I'd hit. My witch

202

magic would probably harm him more than the warlock, but I'd need to use both.

"I don't think so," he said as I tried to skid to a stop.

He lunged, his fist ploughing into my cheek. Paid exploded through my head, my skull rattling as I fell backwards, my arms flailing. Just before I hit the ground, I froze. Oh great, I remembered this trick he'd pulled before.

Coming closer, Vernon laughed as he looked down at me. My spine was arched backwards, my legs bent from the knees. My muscles screeched in pain as he stared. "You're quite remarkable. It's a shame you have to die."

Without saying anything, I felt into mother earth for the impure warlock magic. It flowed into me, heating my insides, almost boiling them. At least I'd never get cold when I had my warlock magic to keep me warm. Although, the intensity of it made my muscles shake.

"Okay," Vernon started.

Before he could go on, I twisted, breaking the weird spell he'd cast on me. My hand touched the earth before I pushed myself up into a stand. My leg kicked out, my knee coming into direct contact with his nether regions. I wasn't usually a fan of taking a man down by hurting his balls, but needs must and all that. Plus, he kinda deserved it.

His grunt was followed by a howl as I grabbed his shoulders and thrust my head towards his, my forehead smacking straight into his nose.

Rubbing my skull as I backed off, I opened my other hand and envisioned a ball of white light. Yes, I was mixing my warlock and witch magic. The threads of dark blue lightning that zinged through the light magic showed that it wasn't just pure.

"I wouldn't if I were you," Vernon said, spitting blood on the ground.

Lifting his arm, he pointed behind me. I didn't look, not daring to take my eyes off my enemy.

"Leave my daughter alone." My father was close, too close.

Why wasn't he in the cairn with the others? How had he got past the barrier spell? He must have come back out once he'd put the others inside, before I'd put the protection spell up. Great.

"Dad, get back inside," I shouted, unable to do anything but hold my magic.

My heart thumped in my chest. My whole body was lined with sweat, small droplets falling down my neck and back.

"We've only got two minutes," Mary called.

Oh crap. I had to get this done. Now.

Without saying any more, I lurched forward, my arms pushing the ball away from me and towards Vernon. His eyes widened as he spun, trying to get out of the way. I hummed deeply as the ball travelled, the size increasing as it went. The link kicked in, making it ten times bigger.

As it smashed into the spirit warlock, it dispersed all over him. He was silent as his body started to go into seizure. He shook violently as his back hit the ground and his eyes rolled into the back of his head. Good.

Spinning, I undid the protection spell so that my mother and Mary could join us. They both rushed over as my father went closer to Vernon. Grabbing my hand, my mother dragged me to the stone.

"Quick, otherwise it will be too late."

Trying to keep a grip on the handle of my dagger as sweat made it slippery, I brought it to my other palm. Slicing quickly, I indicated that my mother should do the spell. She grabbed my hand as blood welled up from the wound. Whispering the spell, she placed my palm flat on the stone's surface.

"Devon!" my father screamed.

Turning, I gasped in a breath. Vernon was standing, his arms around my dad from behind. He held a blade to his throat, a wicked grin on his face. No.

About to rip away from the stone, I struggled when Mary pressed my hand harder. The contact suddenly melded my hand to the stone. I tried to tug away as midnight hit and the spell ignited.

A white mist descended around me as I tried desperately to pull away from the stone. No, if I didn't get to my dad, he would...

Vernon's blade sliced across my father's throat. My father looked at me, his gaze seeking mine. I stared, unable to look away as he mouthed the words 'I love you'. I screamed as the life in his eyes drained, leaving his body with the blood that now drenched his shirt.

"Go," I told the other two as Vernon stepped past my father as he fell and came towards us. "Now."

My mother was on her knees, her head in her hands. She'd watched my father die too. It would be a memory forever ingrained in our minds.

"Mum!"

Stumbling to her feet, my mum grabbed my shoulders. Vernon was taking his time, almost teasing. And, yet, only seconds stretched by.

My body started to shake as the link pulled into the stone.

"I can't leave you," my mum said, grabbing my free hand.

"I can't lose you," I told her.

Mary came around the stone, took my mother's arm and pulled her away. She went, staring after me as I turned my attention back to Vernon. Trying to access my magic, I held my free hand towards him. Nothing came. Except pain. The link was rushing into the stone, taking my energy with it.

"No!" Vernon shouted suddenly as I leant my head against the stone.

I was helpless, unable to do anything to stop him from harming me. But, it was okay. I could join my father with our ancestors. I was ready to leave this life behind. He'd died for me. He was dead.

Arms suddenly wrapped around my legs. Glancing down, I frowned as Vernon clung to me, his arms trying to get a grip. His body was being dragged back by something invisible. Looking up, I released a shuddery breath. My team were standing there, all three of them performing a spell.

They were sending Vernon back to hell. Thank fuck. The pressure grew as Vernon squeezed my legs. What was happening?

I suddenly went lightheaded, the heat from my warlock magic becoming extremely cold. Except for where he held me.

"If I'm going back to hell," he shouted over the vibration of the stone. "I'll take a part of you with me."

Something beneath my feet snapped harshly as Vernon was ripped away from me. Agony resounded through my body as I screamed, my muscles shaking so hard I couldn't hold myself up. My hand was still stuck to the stone, the energy of the link being transferred still rushing through my bones.

Wind swirled around me violently, causing my hair to flick into my eyes. I just made out the image of Vernon being sucked into the ground, back to where he belonged. My father's body lay lifeless on the ground, all alone. Tears streamed down my face as a sucking sensation popped out of my body, and my hand was freed from the stone.

"Fuck," I muttered.

Gerard appeared, wrapping his arms around me as my legs gave way.

"Are you okay?" my man asked, holding me tightly against him. "What happened?"

My body was numb, the pain that had spread through me leaving a trace of something once familiar, but now almost too sore to bear.

"I..." My throat closed at the realisation of what had happened. "I'm no longer a warlock. Vernon severed my link completely, and..." I tried to breathe, but I couldn't catch my breath. "...my dad is dead because of me."

14

Half witch, half... no, no, that's not right. Not anymore. My fingers shook as my mind played what had happened over and over again. My mother sat in the chair beside the bed, her head fallen to the side, her eyes closed in sleep.

Kurt had insisted that I rest in the infirmary. Gerard had refused, bringing me to my bedroom instead. Kingsley had kept me company through the rest of the night, the others coming and going as they dealt with the scene in Scotland.

My father couldn't be dead. I'd told myself that he must be alive. That he was probably in the infirmary. Maybe it was best to go there and see him.

"Are you okay?" My mother's voice caused me to jump.

I'd been about to climb out of bed. "Yes, I just need to go and find dad."

Fresh tears instantly came into her eyes. Oh, crap, I'd ruined that moment of just waking up where you forget all the shit. Her expression made me squeeze my eyes shut. No, there was no going to find dad, he wasn't...

"He died because of me," I whispered, unable to cry.

Numbness made it hard for me to move my arms, even to hold my mother when she shoved to her feet and came to sit on the side of the bed. Not even when she grasped me tight, holding me as close to her as possible.

"It wasn't because of you," she said quietly. "It was because of Vernon Jupiter."

The image of my father's gaze made grief crash through me, bursting down my barriers. Pain lanced harder than my disconnection from impure magic. My whole body shook as I screamed, tears streaming down my face.

Arms were around me, more than one pair. My eyes were closed, unable to see the expression on their faces. All of them. I could smell them as I buried my head into the

211

nearest shoulder. My mother's. Gerard climbed on the bed behind me, putting his arms around me as much as he could. Justina's tears mixed with my own as she kissed my head, stroking my hair. Kurt's breathing was harsh as he flung himself over all of us, somehow managing to stay standing. And, through it all, I only saw the image of my father in my mind, falling to the ground as he mouthed I love you.

We stayed that way for a while, unable to pull apart, unable to do anything but cry. When I could hardly breathe, I managed to untangle myself from my family. Each one of them had wet cheeks. Even Gerard had a snotty nose.

Offering me a tissue, he sat up and pulled me to lean back against him.

"How are you feeling within yourself?" Kurt said. "You know, now you're no longer a warlock?"

Blinking, I tried not to throw a punch in his direction. And, yet, he stood there, as red eyed as the rest of us. Losing my father was a shared grief. They hadn't known my parents for long, but they'd embraced them as much as they had me. Somehow, we'd made this weird family together. And now...

"Mum, I'm so sorry," I whispered, wiping the tears from under her eyes. "How can I make it better?"

Rubbing her face, my mother looked up at the ceiling. "You can just..." Looking back at me, she tilted her head to the side. "...be strong. And, allow yourself to grieve. I..." she almost choked. "...need time to grieve."

Nodding, I tucked her hair behind her ear. She sucked air into her lungs before she climbed off the bed. The others followed, leaving me and Gerard alone. Kingsley squeaked, his hatred of being ignored overwhelming him. Leaning back against my man, I opened my mouth and started to sing. It was a song my father used to sing to me when I was a baby. Kingsley instantly stopped making noise, his little eyes watching me as I waved at him.

Rocking me back and forth, Gerard stayed silent until I'd finished. A part of me was gone completely.

"Not only has my father been taken away from me, I've lost what I did have of him." I hiccupped, swallowing to try and bury the pain.

Gerard's arms tightened around me, his hands coming up to wrap around my shoulders from behind. I was cocooned in his embrace, his scent comforting me as he breathed next to my ear.

"He will always be a part of you," he whispered, kissing my neck gently. "His DNA can never be taken away, and neither can the memories."

"I'm a full Essex witch now."

My statement made me sad somehow. When I'd thought I'd lost my connection to the witch side of me, I'd been distraught. Now that I actually had lost my link to the warlock magic... the warlocks!

"Did it work? Wait... Maxwell, the others. Are they alive? Wow, I've not even asked about them, I-"

"Devon." Sitting up, Gerard shifted so we half faced one another. "Calm down."

Letting out a shaky breath, I leant into him, kissing his chin. He moved my hair back off my sticky face. "The warlocks are fine. They're recovering from Vernon's hit. It might take a few days, but there's no lasting damage. Kurt checked the link. The ritual worked perfectly. Mary's back at home, worried sick about you, but we're keeping her informed."

My energy drained as I sagged against Gerard. He indicated that we should lay down, face to face. I did as he said, looking into his eyes as he stroked my arm. The moment was silent, my body was numb.

"How am I going to support my mother?"

The shock of no longer being half warlock hadn't set in. I'd wanted rid of the main link so badly, I'd almost brought it upon myself.

"You're going to grieve, and then you're going to get up, and help us get Cameron. Your father wanted us to catch him. He was a good man, even if he didn't approve of me."

The tiny quirk of his lips made me smile for a split second. "They'd arranged for me to meet an Essex witch. Although, I think my dad was probably dragged along by my mother."

"They did what?" Gerard went to get up.

Gripping his arm, I forced him to stay with me. Taking a deep breath, he laid back down and settled again.

"You're right," he said, tracing the tattoo of my silhouette on his arm. "This isn't the time to get angry about that."

Sighing, I put my hand over his cheek, tucking my little finger behind his ear. He went still, his gaze intensifying when it met mine.

"I told them that I would never consent to anything because I'm with you. They accepted that."

His tightened jaw relaxed as he put his arm around me. "That's good."

"Vernon was sent back to hell?" My mind was swirling from one thing to the next.

Nodding, Gerard leant forward and kissed my forehead. "Yes. I'm sorry, Devon. I'm so sorry I couldn't be there for you."

Blinking, I swallowed hard when Gerard pulled back. Tears were gathered in his eyes, one sliding out to roll down the side of his face and onto the pillow.

"You've always been there for me."

"No," he exclaimed, rolling onto his back. "I should've been at the ritual, not chasing Cameron Fieldman. If I was there, I could've stopped him. You would been still part warlock. Your father would still be alive."

Wiping my face from the fresh tears that tracked it, I lifted Gerard's arm and snuggled onto his chest. He held me, his breath uneven as he cried silently.

"As a witch, you know that when it's someone's time to die, they do. My father chose to put himself in danger, he chose to help me. I wish he hadn't. I wish I'd checked that he was inside the cairn before I cast the protection spell, but I didn't." Gerard went to lift his head, but I squeezed his waist. "No, I'm not blaming myself either. I'm just saying

216

that what happened was supposed to be. As much as I fucking hate it."

The last part of my sentence was spat harshly. Gerard snorted as he looked down at me. It wasn't in humour, but an emotion between despair and hope.

"We have to live for him now," Gerard said, trying to turn again.

Instead of letting him, I slunk onto his chest, my whole body covering his. He wrapped his arms around me, a question in his raised eyebrows.

"My parents, my father, showed me that love was more important than anything else." I placed my chin on his pec and kept his gaze as I spoke. "I want to live like they did. For each other. For their child. For the good of our community."

"They were kind of heroes. Defying the odds and all that. I'm not sure we can be heroes."

His chest moved as he breathed in. I placed my hand over his heart to feel its beat. "I've fought my feelings for you, I've fought myself. I'm done." Leaning up, I kissed his mouth.

He cradled the back of my head, kissing me back gently. When I pulled away, he blinked quickly. I smiled as I laid my head on his chest and listened to his heartbeat.

"I surrender to you," I breathed. The heavy feeling that dragged my muscles down suddenly lifted. "No matter what happens, we remember him by loving each other until it's no longer right to do so."

Air rushed around my head as he let his breath out. His arms held me to him as I almost melted into his bones.

"I love you, Devon," he whispered. "There will never be a time that I don't."

15

"So, let me get this straight," I said to Kurt as we drove through the streets of London. "You've got one of Cameron's witches from the factory in the back?"

Kurt braked suddenly. My heart jumped in my throat as a cat ran in front of us. Jeez. Who would allow their cat to roam free in London? It was asking for trouble for the poor sweet thing.

"Yeah." Kurt waited patiently for the cat to cross before he moved again. "Justina has made a deal with him. He's agreed to lure Cameron to a meeting in a public place so we can arrest him."

"And what does he get out of it?"

Glancing at me sideways, Kurt raised his eyebrows. "Do you want to get Cameron or not? He gets away with a life sentence instead of a death sentence. Are you sure you're ready for this?"

Sinking back into my seat, I closed my eyes. It had been three days since I'd lost my father, and I couldn't stay in my bedroom any longer. He would've wanted me to catch Cameron Fieldman and stop the witch killings.

"Yes," I said, rubbing my face. "I'm..."

My sentence trailed off as the sunlight came through the window and bathed my whole being. The truth was, I had no idea if I was ready for anything, but I couldn't not live. The distraction would help me to cope. My therapist had visited a couple of times a day since the solstice. I was getting the help I needed. She had even suggested I try to get back to work over the coming weeks. Okay, so it had only been three days, but I was ready to take down the man responsible for so many deaths.

Sighing, Kurt rubbed a hand over his face. "Mackenzie turned up to that meeting with Gerard. He's agreed to testify against Cameron in court."

Looking at him, I shook my head. "Do you think we jumped the gun with them?"

The circumstantial evidence had pointed to the couple, but he had been right. We didn't have hard evidence, although his bomb threat had been completely real, even if it was at Cameron's house. He had led us to believe that we were going to be blown up. That was a crime.

"No." Kurt glanced in the side mirror. "We would've got there in the end. He just didn't help his own cause."

For some reason, I was relieved that Mackenzie had come forward. It helped everyone in the long run and would lead to Cameron's capture. Hopefully.

"When we get to the park..." Kurt switched back to the mission in hand. "...don't show yourself to the witch. Gerard and Justina will get him out."

"I feel bad that Justina is having to sit in the back with them."

Shaking his head, Kurt switched on his indicator and checked that he was clear to drive down towards the park. "Don't worry about it. We don't want him to see you in case he holds a grudge. You did kill his friends."

Ah, yeah, there was that. Well, he shouldn't have been killing people by poisoning Cameron's drugs.

"What do I do?"

Rubbing his hand over his hair, he suddenly looked a little afraid. "Gerard and I will check that the meeting place is clear of other paranormal creatures. We'll then escort him to the bench where the meeting will take place. A barrier spell will be placed around the perimeter. If you feel like helping with that, you can. After that, you need to park the van a couple of streets away."

My gaze snapped to him. "What? I'm driving this beast?"

His sharp nod was followed by a glare. "Don't think I'm happy about it."

A smile came to my lips unbidden. Kurt had never given me such a bitter look before, and it was all over his precious van.

"Don't panic," I said, a wicked grin emerging. "I'll take great care of the beast. If it gets scratched, I'll personally T-cut it out."

"Ha-fucking-ha. As if you'd know how to do that."

Well, he might have that right. I had no idea how to do anything with vehicles. Still, it gave me a tiny bit of joy to see the look of distress on my boss's face. "If you're this bad with an inanimate object, how are you going to cope with me babysitting your kid?"

His bark of laughter made me glare this time.

"As if I'd leave my baby with you."

"Huh!" I exclaimed. "I'll have you know that I'm amazing with animals."

His frown made me laugh. "Are you calling my child an animal?"

The implication hadn't crossed my mind. Hilarity rose up my throat before I could stop it. The giggles overtook as Kurt shook his head, making it worse. "No, I meant that if I'm good with animals, I'll be good with children."

Sighing, Kurt pulled up in a layby next to the park. "Not sure of your reasoning there, but we'll see."

"When you're wanting some one on one time with your woman, you'll let me babysit, you wait. You'll practically be begging."

His face finally cracked into a smile. "I'll be begging both you and Justina by then. Wait, what... No, I'll be begging you to look after the kid and Justina for-"

"Okay!" I put my hand up, stopping him from going on. "I get it. Let's get back to the present, shall we?"

Straightening his expression when the back door opened, Kurt looked at me. "It's good to see you smile." Ducking me under the chin, he cleared his throat. "So, you'll park the van in an underground car park not far from here. I've put it in the sat nav for you. After that, you'll join us in that bush behind the bench. We'll need to hide ourselves with an invisibility spell."

My gaze followed his pointed finger. Ah, okay. So, we had to literally go into a bush? Since when did our stakeouts involve nature? Not that I was adverse to it, I loved mother earth. However, a bush wouldn't exactly be the perfect vantage point.

A sudden knock on the window made me jump. Gerard's face appeared, his bright green eyes looking between us. Opening the door, I let him help me out. They had to prepare the area before the undercover witch could get out. Justina stood beside the van, a questioning look on her face.

"Did we hear you laughing?" she asked as I went over.

The others walked towards the bench, their heads turning to see who was around. It was just after lunchtime in the middle of the week, which meant there were several people lazing in the park. We would have to protect the whole area so that no one saw what was happening.

"You did hear me laugh. Kurt doesn't seem to trust me with his van... or the baby."

Cocking her head, she smiled. "Well, I trust you with both. Although," she said, gesturing at the park. "I'm not sure this is such a good idea." Justina absentmindedly stroked her stomach as she spoke.

The tiny bump that showed made a lump come to my throat. I was basically going to be an aunt. I couldn't wait.

Leaning against the van, I checked around us. The tooting of the cars kept making me jump. To say I was slightly on edge was an understatement. However, I was ready. "I'm sure it will be fine. You've planned everything out perfectly."

"I don't mean the meeting," Justina said, placing a hand on my shoulder. "I mean you."

"I'm not missing it for anything. If I don't throw myself into my work, I'm going to get extremely depressed."

"We're ready," Gerard announced as he marched across the grass towards us.

Kurt was standing by the meeting point, his arms folded. Our scene was set up, ready for action. In the van behind me, the witch who had survived my fire was waiting.

"Cameron might be watching the place, so we need to hurry up," Justina said.

If he was, surely he wouldn't come? Although, if he cared about his coven at all, he would check on the witches who had been running his underground drug ring.

Opening the door, Gerard went inside the van. I stood back, out of sight. The man might have had an adverse reaction if he saw me. I did burn some of his mates to death. My bad.

"You know your cue?" Justina asked me quietly as Gerard dragged the witch out.

Ducking to the front of the vehicle, I threw a thumbs up to Justina before I opened the door and jumped into the driver's seat. Yes, I was finally driving Kurt's beloved truck. Frowning when I tried to reach the pedals, I froze. When I was a child, my father had sat me on his lap when he drove. He often joked that I might never be able to reach the pedals. It was a memory that I'd completely forgotten.

Grief flooded me as I switched the engine on and almost stood to place my foot on the accelerator. It was a good job the thing was automatic, or I would never have been able to move it.

Almost crashing into a car as I pulled out, I laughed when I saw Kurt put his arms on either side of his head as he watched me. What was he worried about? I was literally moving it two streets away before I joined them at our agreed location.

Slamming the brakes on when the traffic light turned red, I cursed. Driving in London was a nightmare. No wonder Kurt never wanted anyone else to do it. It took a certain level of concentration that I didn't have. Especially when I was fighting back the tears because of my dad.

When the green light flashed on, I glanced to my left. My foot pushed the accelerator when I saw Cameron Fieldman striding towards the park. Shit. He was early.

Grabbing out my phone, I steered the van onto the next street. My hands fumbled as I turned the wheel and dialled Justina at the same time.

"Don't tell me," Kurt answered. "You crashed?"

"No. I just saw Cameron. He'll be there in a few minutes. Get out of there!"

His sharp "copy that" was followed by a beep in my ear. He was gone. Shit, I had to hurry the fuck up. If I wasn't there in time, I'd miss out on all the action. Not only that, if Cameron thought it was a trap, he'd disappear. My link to the ley line might be the only thing that would catch him. The others were powerful, but the ley line magic was unbeatable. They needed me.

The tyres of the van skidded as I turned into the next road. Swinging it around the corner, I squeaked as the underground car park entrance came into view. Slowing down, I took a deep breath and managed to manoeuvre the fairly big vehicle under the height restriction post and find a parking space that was empty either side. I needed all the room I could get to reverse the bugger.

Getting out, I locked the van before walking back up through the entrance. The rips in my jeans made the air tickle my skin. My thin T-shirt was not enough coverage in the shade of the building. Goosebumps erupted on my arms as I checked around, my hair flying out behind me. There wasn't anyone about. Good.

"Here goes," I whispered, feeling for my witch magic.

It slowly filtered up as I chanted an invisibility spell before I flashed to Gerard's side.

"Shit!" he exclaimed as I landed in the bush beside him. "You scared me."

Smiling, I took his hand. He'd been scratching the stubble on his jaw, obviously nervous. Justina and Kurt were standing on the other side of him, their gaze trained on the man who sat on the bench. He had his back to us. It was rigid as he kept his gaze forward. He was anxious. It was obvious from the tap of his foot on the ground. I was about to speak when Cameron came through the entrance of the park.

"This is it," Kurt said. "When I say go, we all approach from behind. The witch must be protected at all times. Cameron comes with us, dead or alive."

Chewing on the inside of my cheek, I couldn't take my gaze away from the magnetic mob coven leader. He strode forward when he caught sight of the witch. It was pretty risky to be hiding in the bushes that he now faced. Hopefully, he wouldn't detect the invisibility spells that were active around all of us.

The witch stood as Cameron approached. Offering his hand, Cameron went stiff when the man shook it. Oh, shit, it looked like he knew something was up.

"I'm sorry about what happened. How's everyone doing?" Sitting on the bench, he patted the seat next to him.

As the witch lowered himself, Cameron tucked a hand into his suit jacket pocket. I was the only one who could see the left side of him. The bulge in his pocket made me swallow. No, not because I was thinking naughty things about bulges, but because he had a weapon of some sort.

"He knows," I whispered to Gerard.

The others glanced at me, frowns on their face. They had heard me. The energy was thick with suspense, especially now the attention was on me, instead of the suspect.

Gesturing with my blade, I forced them to turn their focus back to our goal. Where had my dagger come from? I must've been so wrapped up in the job, I'd automatically got it out without thinking. I did that way too much nowadays.

"Some of them died. The bitch who did it got her comeuppance though," the witch said.

Ah, yeah, I'd forgotten how much they probably hated me, even though they were bloody murderers, the hypocrites.

Cameron lounged back against the wooden bench, his hand still in his pocket. "I met her once," he said, running a hand over his long hair. "She was full of pent up deliciousness that needed to be released. What happened to her?"

My swallow was audible, or certainly to me, anyway. Gerard glanced at me, his expression clear. Yeah, the mob leader had pheromones pumping out, even now. He must've known that I was in the vicinity. He wouldn't say something so-

"She's no longer a half-breed."

The pain that gripped my chest made me open my mouth to suck in a breath. Jeez, even the bastard witch could hurt me with the truth.

"How the fuck did that happen?" Cameron demanded, leaning forward.

Wow, he really had been in hiding the last few days. That wasn't exactly a bad thing. Anyway, how did the witch know about my unfortunate circumstances?

Glancing at Justina, I glared when she shrugged an apology. She had told the man so he could gain Cameron's trust. That wasn't going to fucking work when the runaway already knew that we were here. Pushing my ire down, I clenched my free hand and waited for Cameron's move. If the

others didn't believe me, then I had to be ready.

Sitting forward as he leant his elbows on his knees, the witch looked sideways at his boss. "Some evil spirit warlock basically ripped out her link to magic. She's just an Essex witch now."

"There's no such thing as *just* an Essex witch," Cameron said. "They're more powerful than any of us. If they know how to use the ley lines. Still, I'd like to help her to unleash all that... frustration."

Shuddering, I ignored Gerard when he narrowed his gaze on me. His annoyance wasn't aimed at me, but he knew Cameron couldn't see the flick of jealousy that crossed his face. Why was he worried? As if I would ever allow the creep that killed witches to get close to me.

Sitting back again, Cameron whipped something out of his left pocket. His right arm stretched out behind the witch, his fingers wrapping around the back of the man's neck.

"If you don't come out now," he shouted. "I'll slice this man's throat."

A knife was held in the air, the sun reflecting off the silver metal. My planned retort was cut short when the others thrust out from the bushes without even looking in my direction. I almost tripped as I followed, my haste making me clumsy. Who was I kidding? I was the clumsiest agent in the field. Probably ever.

"Ah," Cameron exclaimed, jumping to his feet. He dragged the witch with him, not even bothering to apologise for using the man to lure us out. "I can feel you, but I can't see you. Don't be cowards, now."

Glancing at Justina, I raised my eyebrows. Cameron was looking around, trying to work out where we were. Nodding her head to the side, Justina indicated that we move around to the front of the bench so there was plenty of space around us.

"Freeze!" she said forcefully as she revealed herself.

We followed suit, each one of us becoming visible. The other three held their guns high, aimed directly at Cameron as he spun towards us. My dagger was by my side, ready for action, but not instantly threatening. There was no point. Three guns was enough to keep him under control.

"There she is, the famous Essex witch. I'm sorry to hear about your unfortunate mishap. I can't even begin to understand how it feels to lose a part of yourself." The criminal watched me, his face clear of expression.

And, yet, I knew he was being genuine. Why did he have such an interest in me? And, why the hell did his words warm me slightly? Because of the darkness in him. The darkness I had lost with the warlock link.

"You might as well give up now, Cameron," Gerard called. "We have you surrounded."

The witch glared at my boyfriend, his cheeks turning pink. "Ah, the light witch. The one who torments himself because of past mistakes. It's good to see that you've healed a lot of your broody bullshit. And, the famous agent pair," he said, looking at Justina and Kurt. "So revered in your field. Congratulations, by the way."

A shiver ran over me. He had done his research, and considering we were top agents, he'd uncovered much more than he should've done. Maybe the government had let him know more than they'd realised. How had they believed the cold hearted murderer?

"Why did you kill all those people?" I blurted.

As I caught his attention, Cameron lowered the knife to his side. He was ready to talk, or was he keeping us distracted?

The hairs on my arm stood up as I linked into the ley line. Allowing myself to relax into the magic, I almost gasped at the difference. Now that my warlock link was gone, my pure magic was expansive. I could push the energy out of me, almost scanning for... something. I wasn't sure what.

"Because my sister is in love with a warlock. I had to stop them. As much as I admire you, I don't want my sister arrested because of her foolishness. Being in love with another paranormal species is illegal."

He had a point. A big one. However, he hadn't answered my question. "I'm sorry," I said, stepping in front of the others. "How does that justify killing tons of humans and witches?"

His mouth opened, showing his gritted teeth. It was obviously a touchy subject for him, which was strange. He had seemed completely emotionally distant. What was driving him to act this way?

"If Mackenzie's locked away, they'll both be safe. I had to do something drastic to make sure he'll never be freed."

Wait. Cameron had excused his behaviour as a protection mechanism for both Mackenzie and Candy?

The others shuffled on their feet. They were getting agitated. The longer we kept him talking, the harder it would be to get the job done. We had to take him in, one way or another. However, the threat against the witch who we'd sworn to protect stopped us from just shooting him.

"I understand," I said, keeping my gaze locked on his. "You love your sister."

Nodding, he shifted to the right slightly, his gaze going just above my head. He was waiting for someone. Pushing my energy further out, I coughed when the magical imprints of several other witches, all in a circle around us, alerted me to their presence.

Turning my head to the side, but keeping my eye on Cameron, I quietly spoke to my team. "We've got company."

"I'm sorry." Cameron glanced at the witch. "I knew that this was a set up. My contacts told me that every witch had been caught. When you tried to trick me into believing that Lucas here got away, I knew what was happening. I came because I need to end this chase and get back to my life."

The click of my colleagues guns made me glance over my shoulder. The others frowned as each magazine dropped out of the handles of their gun, thumping on the ground below. Shit, they'd just been disarmed.

Several witches, both male and female, approached us, their hands held out. They were casting a barrier spell, their bodies the boundary.

"It's okay," Cameron said, pointing directly at me. "I just want to deal with you."

My friends spun as several witches appeared out of nowhere and came at them. I stepped back as Gerard engaged with one of them, whacking his gun over the enemy's head.

The witch's head snapped back, but he kept coming, throwing his fists into Gerard's side.

About to go to his defence, I stopped when Justina grunted. Shit, no. She should not be fighting. If she was hit in the stomach, she could lose the-

"Leave that one alone!" Cameron ordered as a witch ploughed his fist into my boss's face. "She's pregnant."

Instantly backing off, the witch howled when Justina cast a freezing spell. His hands turned to blocks of ice, forcing him to drop to the ground.

"What do you want?" I snarled as I faced Cameron.

He still held the witch. The man was squirming, his little beady eyes begging me to help him. As if I cared what happened to a man who had no regard for those he had harmed. Not just the people he had killed, but the families they'd left behind.

"I told you, I need to be free of you so I can go back to my life. You need to arrest Mackenzie. Lock him up for life, and then, I'll let your friends go."

My insides quivered in rage as my skin heated. The group of witches had captured the other agents and were marching them towards our enemy. Gerard shook his head when I went to move towards them. It was a warning. He wanted me to engage Cameron. For some reason, he had some kind of fascination with me. Maybe I could use that to my advantage.

"Okay," I said, tucking my dagger away and holding up my hands in surrender. "I don't have the power to do what you say, only Justina does."

"You have all the power." He released the witch, shoving him to one of his cronies.

They had grown in number, roughly fifteen of them now surrounded us. Some casting the barrier spell, others now holding my friends.

"I'm nowhere near as powerful as I was. You need to let them go so they can do what you ask." My hands were shaking slightly. My first foray into the field without my warlock magic was intimidating. Especially now I was face to face with a powerful mob coven leader who had it in his head that I could make decisions. I'd never been good when I had to make a choice. Did he not know that? It had taken me almost ten thousand years to decide whether I wanted to be leader of the warlocks. And, I'd never got round to deciding whether I was going to be a witch or a warlock. That was taken out of my hands. Huh. Maybe that meant it was time to take my life back, and make the bloody decisions.

"No!" I almost shouted as he went to speak. "I will not bow down to you. I'm sick and tired of running away, of trying to be diplomatic. Sorry," I said to Justina who just shrugged. "I will not be pushed around anymore. I am fucking powerful."

A big smirk spread across Cameron's face. "See, I told you I could open you up. Can't you see how amazing we'd be together? You, with all that ley line magic. Me, teaching you how to use it. Between us, we'd be able to take over the world. If we wanted to."

Flames licked my stomach as he leered at me. Er, what was happening? Was the man coming on to me? If he was, it was extremely creepy.

Gerard thrust his elbow back into his captor's gut, bringing the man to the ground. Whipping my dagger out when Cameron was distracted, I crouched down and held the tip to the earth, right where the ley line rested underneath. I hadn't noticed how strong it vibrated beneath my feet when we'd first arrived.

Using my dagger now, I could access the magic directly, without bringing it through me. My body had weakened the link, but now I could finally wield the dagger properly.

"STOP!" I cried, drawing everyone's attention to me.

Several witches had pounced on Gerard, forcing him to comply. He stopped struggling when he heard me, his gaze connecting with mine. A small smile came to his lips. I winked quickly as Cameron looked at me.

Holding his hand out when the other witches' feet went to step forward, he swallowed hard. His eyes widened as he watched the flicker of pure white flames travel from the ground, over and up my dagger. Instead of sinking into the metal, it carried on up my arm. The sensation was tickly as it engulfed my body, setting me alight with magic I had never been able to access.

"Shit," I muttered, looking at Kurt. "You'll have to perform that spell on me after all this has ended. This kind of power is addictive."

Cameron slowly came forward. Stretching up into a normal stand, I held the dagger in front of me. Would he fight me? He would be a fool to think that his tainted magic would be a match for mine.

"I need you in my life." His legs were moving, his arms outstretched.

A crazed look entered his eyes as I ran backwards, trying to keep him at bay. He had been right about me not knowing how to use the ley line magic properly. I was worried that by using it now, I would hurt my friends.

Somehow, I managed to stay on my feet until my back bashed into the wall of protection. A hiss pushed through my clenched teeth when the heat from the spell seared the back of my bare arms.

"I'm still trying to be diplomatic," I said as I side-tracked, dodging a witch who held the spell.

Launching himself, Cameron came for me. Ducking, I spun away, swiping my dagger through the arm of his jacket. He howled as the tip of the blade sliced his skin.

The other agents had engaged in fighting again. There was no way I could expect them to not join in. And, yet, what if the magic overtook again? I had to hold back if I wanted them to survive. After seeing what I was capable of at the factory, I was on edge, unable to release my full power.

"I will have your magic," Cameron screamed as he held his arm.

Opening his mouth wide, he recited an ancient spell. One that I recognised straight away. It was the one my mother had used to transfer the warlock link from me to the tree. He was trying to steal my link to the ley line.

"Devon!" Gerard shouted. "No more diplomacy!"

Ducking out of the way when another witch threw a knife at me, I tried to conjure a ball of magic. My heart sank when the impure magic didn't come. Shit, I had to focus all my energy on my witch magic.

"*Incendia!*" Lighting the witch on fire was the quickest way to get him off my back.

Cameron's whole body started to shake as other witches came for me. They were going to hold me still so he could do the spell. No, I wouldn't let him. Anyway, how could he...?

Bringing his hand away from where I'd cut him, Cameron grinned. A tiny spark of bright white magic had obviously been left behind by the dagger. He was using that as a focal point.

Closing my eyes, I focused on Gerard, Justina and Kurt. Their fighting grunts made me shake, my body wanting to protect them. Hopefully, they would forgive me for what I was about to do.

Whispering a transportation spell, I sent the three of them back to the agency building. My eyes snapped open as soon as the startled cry of those fighting them reached me. A hand was coming towards me. Spinning, I swiped my dagger down, cutting the woman's wrist clean through.

My lover and bosses were nowhere to be seen. Good, they would at least be protected, even if they hated me for the rest of my life.

An arm came around me from behind, grabbing the wrist that held my dagger. Dropping it, I laughed when I caught the

243

handle in my free hand. Spinning the blade, I shoved it backwards, straight into his groin. I was released as a sharp intake of breath resounded in my ear before the scream followed. Served him fucking right.

"Stop fighting me!" Cameron squeezed through his teeth.

His whole body shook as he stayed where he stood, rooted to the ground beneath him. Mother earth was a bitch to manipulate, especially when the witch trying to command her didn't have Essex blood in his veins.

"You need to stop fighting me. I told you, I'm done with being diplomatic. Call your witches off, and you can live the rest of your days in prison." My chest rose and fell rapidly, the fight taking all of my energy.

For some reason, I wanted him to give up. I didn't want to kill all of the witches who were in the vicinity. I was done with harming others because of my job. Although, they hadn't given a flying fucktard when they had poisoned the drugs. Maybe I was being too nice.

Something hit me in the shoulder, jerking my dagger arm forward. Pain forced the air out of my lungs, making me turn to see what it was. Shit, a huge brick was laying on the floor behind me. Seriously? Why were they throwing stones?

Flicking my wrist, I chanted a quick entrapment spell. Vines came up from the ground, instantly catching the witch who had dislocated my shoulder.

The pain made me blink as I suddenly felt a tugging on the earth beneath my feet. My magic slowly started to recede. No. I wouldn't let that bastard take what was mine. I had already been violated in that way, it wasn't going to happen again.

My boots were smashing on the ground before I could think. Cameron was only a few yards from me. Why wasn't he moving?

Glancing at his feet, I clocked the small glow on the grass. What the fuck?

"Bitch!" A witch screamed as I passed.

She reached out, scraping her nails down my elbow in an attempt to capture me. Cringing, I kept going, my eyes tracing the position of the witches who held us in the circle. They were holding candles, the flames flickering madly as they joined in Cameron's spell. I hadn't even noticed that they had formed a pentagram.

Cameron grinned as I came closer, my dagger extended, even though my arm was extremely weak. Holding his hands in the air, he opened himself up for attack. And yet, I knew better. He would have a barrier spell around him.

Weapons flew at me from all angles, but I ducked and dived. As soon as I reached the leader, I came to a halt. He winked at me, his smug grin making my skin heat so hot, it was as if my warlock magic was back.

"I'm sorry to do this to you." The weapons stopped coming as he waved the others away.

The pull was still strong, my witch magic being disconnected from my DNA. I swallowed hard as I stared into his eyes. They were dark, the irises blurring with the black of his pupils.

"I finally know who I am," I whispered. "Devon Jinx, witch, no longer warlock, whatever."

Raising my dagger hand, I took a deep breath. Cameron just smirked, knowing full well I couldn't penetrate his wall. A shorter witch ran at me, diving for my legs. Crouching, I winked at Cameron as I jumped as high as I could, using the witch's back as leverage. He skidded away, his face scraping the earth.

A war cry escaped me as I fell.

Grasping my dagger in both hands, I faced it downwards and plunged it into the earth as I landed in a crouch, just in front of Cameron's feet.

The ground vibrated as the blade cut the cord that Cameron had been trying to create. My hair was in my eyes as a flash of brilliant light zipped up the blade, through me and flew out in all directions, knocking down every single witch inside the circle. Looking up from where I knelt on the ground, I smirked at Cameron as he grasped his chest. Falling to his knees directly in front of me, he gasped for breath. His gaze was glued to mine, his eyes unblinking as his life no doubt flashed before his eyes.

"Don't fuck with an Essex witch. Especially one who now knows how to use the ley line." A tiny pang of regret filtered through me as he collapsed to the side, his chest going still and his hands going limp.

I wasn't sad because I'd just killed all of the witches around me. I was sad because I'd felt the magic of the ley line, but I had to let it go. Not because of Gerard, but because of how I felt for him. Others might believe that magic and materialistic things made them happy, but I knew that connection far outweighed any of it. And, I would do anything to be with those I loved.

16

"Mum," I said as I gripped her hands. "There's something I need to tell you." The time had come.

The team had managed to get back to the park not long after I'd broken the spell that Cameron had been casting. I'd been on one knee, staring at my dagger where it was wedged into the ground. Gerard had pulled me into a stand, hugging me so tightly, I could hardly breathe.

"What is it?" my mother asked, concern spreading across features that were so like mine.

It had been a week since I'd taken Kurt's dead or alive order for Cameron seriously. I hadn't even been aware that blasting the ley line would cause it to thrust through me before going back into the earth. It just so happened that the magic was powerful enough to kill any living creature in the vicinity. My stomach dropped at the memory of bodies that had laid around me. Killing people, even those who were criminals, made me want to vomit. It was fortunate that there hadn't been any innocent people around that day. Guilt was already a bugger to bear, but loss of innocent life would've marked my soul.

As I brought myself back to the present, I swallowed hard and looked up at my mother. Fiddling with the hem of my black summer dress... Yes, I sometimes wore dresses... I patted the bench in the tiny courtyard at the back of the agency building, indicating that my mother should join me. I had never taken advantage of the pretty little area, but my mother often sat outside reading. That's where I had found her only moments before.

"I'm disconnecting from the ley line," I started, not pausing to give my mum time to reply. "The ancestors told Mary that I had to marry an Essex witch if I wanted to keep my link. Obviously, Gerard's not an Essex witch, so I've made the decision to give up my heritage. I've spoken to Becky, my seer friend, and she's seen it done before."

My hands were slick with sweat as my mother dropped them. Sighing to herself, she stared at the hard stone paving slabs under our feet. The thump of my heartbeat was faster than usual. I was scared. My mother had been gloriously happy when she'd realised that I could still connect to the ley line, even though I had warlock blood. To give it up hadn't been something I'd taken lightly.

"I'm not surprised. I've been waiting for you to tell me." Her eyes were clouded when she glanced at me. "Your father guessed it a long time ago."

The sudden lump in my throat made me cough. We'd had his funeral yesterday. Saying goodbye to him had been the hardest thing I'd ever had to do. Especially as it was for real this time. Gerard had held me all night long, allowing me to sob, to laugh about the memories of my childhood, or to just be silent. It was in those silent moments, when he held space for me to be who I was, I'd decided it was time. There was no point in holding off the inevitable.

"I miss him," I whispered, smiling to myself when a small white feather floated down to land on the ground in front of us.

"He's here." My mother took my hand and laid it on her leg, a soft expression coming over her face. "I can feel him."

A sob escaped my mouth before I could pull it back. My mother moved to cradle me against her, guiding my head so it rested on her chest. As her hand stroked my hair, she sang the song my father had always sang to me, just like I had with Gerard the night my father died.

"I fully support your wish to be with Gerard." Her words were quiet, said directly after she'd finished the song. "Just like your father did."

"He did?" Pulling away to look at her, I ignored the sound of London city in the distance.

The sun was bright as it caressed my skin, warming me to the bone. The energy did feel like my father's, I had to admit.

"I was the one who wanted you to meet the Essex witch. He told me that you had chosen your match and that I shouldn't interfere. He was right."

Wow. My father had approved of Gerard? That was something I didn't realise, even if I knew deep down that my mother was the one who had instigated the whole arranged marriage bullshit.

"Gerard will be pleased to know that he wasn't hated by dad."

"Or me," she said quickly as she bent to pick up the feather. "I've always liked Gerard. I just wanted you to enjoy your heritage. Being disconnected from the ley line drove your grandmother crazy. However, it's none of my business. You're a very different person to Helena. You're strong, Devon."

My little laugh made her look at me. I was extremely different to my grandmother, but was I strong? Sometimes I wasn't so sure. A lot of paranormal creatures had placed me on a pedestal, even Cameron. For a long time, I fought to be accepted, but fighting wasn't the answer. Surrender was.

"I love my life," I said, looking up at the agency building. "I'm lucky to have found my friends, my man, and a job I love. I even got my parents back from the dead."

Frowning at myself, I shook my head. What a thing to say. My mother laughed gently, patting my knee.

"Tact has never been your thing, my dear." Standing, she leant over and kissed me on the head. "Let's get going, then."

Looking around, I pretended to look innocent. "Going where?"

Putting her hands on her hips, my mother raised her eyebrows as she looked down at me. "Firstly, you're not patient."

Getting up, I linked my arm through hers. "Okay..."

"Secondly, you've been planning something with the others over the last few days, so I'm in no doubt it will happen soon. You're the queen of putting things off until the last minute, which is why I'm guessing that the unlinking is happening today."

Oh boy, my mother knew better than I realised. Once Kurt had cast the spell on me to disassociate magic with feeling good, I'd wanted to be free of the ley line link. Not because I no longer wanted it. In fact, since I'd used it properly, I wanted it more than ever, even with the spell. It was because I wanted to get used to life as a normal witch. One who had to retrain to build her strengths again.

"I love you," I said, kissing her on the cheek as we went into the kitchen.

The others were there, waiting patiently. Justina cradled her small stomach pouch. Kurt had his arm thrown over her shoulders, his fingers on the other hand drumming on the work surface next to him. Gerard was behind, his gaze staring off into the distance.

He only realised we were there when Justina cleared her throat.

"I'm not able to join you straight away," she said, her face devoid of any expression. "There's something I need to do. I'll be there though."

Smiling at her, I nodded. That was fine. As long as she was there to support me when the ritual was done, I didn't mind her being late.

"It's okay..." My mother nudged me gently in the ribs. "...I'm here for my baby girl."

Smiling, I looked at Gerard. The movement of his throat showed me that he was nervous. I didn't blame him, my stomach was infested with butterflies.

Justina turned to Kurt to give him a quick kiss. Leaving his side, she approached Gerard. Leaning up, she put her arms around his neck and whispered something in his ear. He flinched as she pulled away and almost rushed from the room. Was she okay?

Rubbing his neck, Gerard frowned to himself. I was tempted to ask what was wrong, but Kurt strode over and took my hand. Gesturing for Gerard to join us, he whispered a transportation spell.

"Oh good," he remarked dryly when we landed in Becky's back garden. "They've made it pretty."

The disgust that laced his voice made me giggle. As a seer, Becky knew how to create a gorgeous garden. The unlit fairy lights that hung across trees and over a wooden gazebo were beautiful. Dusk was coming so the lights would look stunning when it got dark. I wasn't going to complain, not when I was about to play out one of the biggest moments in my life.

"The flowers are..." My mother's sentence trailed off.

Vines climbed up the gazebo. The colours of the little flowers were a gorgeous contrast to the green. The sheer white curtains that hung from the sides were pegged back to give the whole place a soft and floaty feel. Flower beds were dotted along the gravel pathway that led to where Becky now stood in the shade of the gazebo.

Gerard followed behind as my mum dragged me up to greet Becky. I wanted to talk to him, to check that he was okay, and to find out what Justina had said to make him cringe.

"I'm so happy to see you!" Becky exclaimed, throwing her arms around me.

Although it had been a while since she'd helped me, we had kept in contact. She'd been extremely supportive in my choice to disconnect from the ley line. However, she wasn't able to perform the ritual, only another Essex witch could do that.

"Devon." Gemma Abbott greeted me when I nodded in her direction.

She had agreed to help. Her judgement was held on by a string, I could see it in the way she almost tutted when Gerard came into the shelter.

My foot almost knocked over a candle as I stood back. There was a pentagram on the floor, made out of salt. An unlit candle sat on the edge of each star point. Anxiety rushed through me as I saw the small circle in the middle. It was where I was going to stand as my link to the ley line was severed.

"I've brought a witness," I said to my mum as Theresa, the leader of the London witch coven, stepped in behind Gerard.

She smiled at Gemma, greeting her with a warm hug. Why hadn't the woman ever been nice to me like that? Oh yeah, because I'd been a hybrid.

Turning to my mother, Theresa embraced her gently. "I'm sorry," she whispered as she let her go.

My fists clenched at the same time as Gerard's jaw. Reaching out to him, I threaded my fingers through his. She was probably talking about my father, not the fact that I was breaking tradition.

"Gerard," I said to make him look at me.

He stared at the ground, blinking rapidly as he took a deep breath. When he lifted his gaze, it softened as soon as it landed on me. My whole body was shaking, my breath short. I wasn't exactly ecstatic about what was about to happen either, but I wasn't just doing it for him.

Leaning up, I grabbed the back of his head and pulled him closer. He bent down so I could whisper in his ear. "I love you, but I'm not doing this for you. This is for me. I chose my own destiny, and that includes who I end up with."

A small smile lifted the corners of his lips. His bright green eyes stared into my soul, asking for permission to be let in. I kept my gaze steady on his, allowing him to see what he could. My wall was down, my heart open, my determination strong.

His tattooed arms came around me as he pulled me close. The light touch of his lips against mine made me shudder, especially when I opened my eyes to see him watching me. Wow. He was as open to me as I was to him. Mr Sexy Open Heart was even sexier than he'd ever been before.

"Can we get on with this?" Kurt interrupted.

He had been speaking to Gemma, updating her on the write up of Cameron's final moments. She'd felt the pull on the ley line and launched an investigation into it. The results had been quick and swift. I'd used the ley line for protection purposes only. That was covered in the rule of ley line use apparently. Who knew?

Becky stepped forward. "Yes, we can. Devon. Can I ask you to stand in the circle, please?"

Bending forward, Becky let her messy blonde hair tumble around her. Taking a deep breath, she brought her arms up to the side and stood up straight, her eyes closed.

Stroking Gerard's face, I left him to do as the seer had asked. It was time to let go. I was ready. Even if my body vibrated like it was on a fast spin.

"I love you," my mum said as I held my arms by my side.

"So serious." Kurt tried to smile. "Don't worry, I'll train you in herbology."

Shaking my head, I pretended to scowl at him. "Great, I'll be a bloody useless witch then."

"Well, at least Kingsley can be your familiar now." He brought the little fella out of his pocket, winking when I put a hand to my chest.

My little best friend made noises as he wiggled his whiskers. To be able to connect to him as a familiar may very well be possible now that I was a complete witch. That was something that hadn't even crossed my mind.

"The dagger," Becky said loudly.

Each of us snapped to attention. It was time. My hands shook so badly, I struggled to grasp the handle of my weapon as I pulled it out of my jacket pocket. Laying it down on the ground in front of me, I sucked back a sob. It was almost like saying goodbye to Kingsley, although nowhere near as painful as that would be. Still, the dagger was my baby. My weapon.

"Gemma will cut the tie to the link once she's invoked the spell that highlights it. Only Essex witches can see the line, so if everyone else could stay silent throughout this ceremony, it would be much appreciated."

For once, I didn't have a quip, or snarky comment. Tears slowly traced down my face as Becky gestured for me to kneel. Glancing at Gerard, I smiled when he mouthed that he loved me. He wasn't the reason I was giving myself up, but he sure as hell was a good motivator for me to take control of my life.

"Gemma," Becky said. "If you could enter the circle and start the spell."

Nodding once, the kickass gorgeous agent stepped over the salt and came to stand in front of me. Her brown hair moved in the breeze as she bent to pick up the dagger. "You've very brave," she whispered, her gaze strong as she gave me a very slight nod.

Closing my eyes, I clenched my hands into fists to stop them shaking. Images of the last few months played through my mind. Fighting warlocks, switching over the leadership to Maxwell, my grandmother kidnapping me, and finally Cameron. All those who had tried to take me down had failed. I was sure that there would be many more. And, yet, I wasn't afraid. Losing my link to the ley line wasn't the end of the world. I would rebuild my witch magic again. I would train in combat, and maybe even bloody herbology.

Gemma took a deep breath and started a spell in Latin. Containing the tears that dribbled down my face was impossible. Regardless of how ready I was, a part of me wished it could be another way.

The sound of the blade of my dagger sliding across her skin made me flinch. No one had ever cut themselves with my weapon. Well, no one that I hadn't intentionally attacked.

"Stop!!" Justina suddenly appeared at the entrance to the gazebo, her hand held in the air as silence fell.

Blinking, I looked at her. My heart was about to go into cardiac arrest. What was she doing?

Gemma stepped back out of the circle, holding her hand away so her blood didn't drip within the pentagram.

"What's the matter?" Kurt demanded.

Gerard stepped closer, his frown dragging his eyebrows low. I stared, my mouth open as I waited. It wasn't like my boss to be firstly, late, and secondly, dramatic.

"It's okay," I said, rubbing my cheeks. "You haven't missed it."

Justina was panting as if she'd been running. "Good," she breathed.

Everyone looked at one another, clearly as confused as I was.

Leaning over, Justina grabbed Gerard's arm for support.

"I'm not happy that I didn't miss it." She panted. "I'm here to stop it!"

Scrambling to my feet, I was about to go to her. Becky held out a hand to stop me, her gaze pointed at the star. Oh right, I couldn't go out of the circle, or I would ruin the spell.

Kurt came over and took Justina's hand. "What's going on? You need to hurry up and tell us. Don't leave us hanging."

Her small laugh made me smile. They made the perfect couple. Even when she punched him softly in the ribs, he just shrugged.

"You might not have to do this. I took a blood sample from Gerard just before you came here. I've been doing some research to find out if there's a way for you to stay connected to the ley line. Just before you came into the kitchen earlier, I got a message from a contact who does ancestry investigations."

Looking at Gerard, Justina placed a hand on his cheek. Perspiration broke out over my body. What was she talking about? Why would she take a blood sample from Gerard?

"Clearly you found something out." Gerard rubbed his arm, right where the tattoo of my silhouette was. The small reminder of how much I meant to him made me tear up again. My emotions were getting out of control. I would need ten thousand therapy sessions after today.

"Gerard, your great, great, great grandfather was the illegitimate child of Abraham Abbott."

"No fucking way!" Gemma exclaimed, marching around the circle.

I hadn't even noticed the documents in Justina's hand until Gemma took them from her. I stared, unable to say a word. Unable to take it in. Was he...? Did that make him...?

"It's true," Gemma whispered as she read the paper. "You're an illegitimate heir of the same Essex line as my father's."

My hand covered my mouth as my stomach rolled. What did that mean? If Gerard had Essex witch DNA that meant...

Spinning on his heel, Gerard faced Becky. He didn't even look at me. "Can you ask the ancestors if this is legit? Will they let me marry Devon if it's true?"

To say I was about to be sick was probably an understatement. My fate rested on my ancestors. Spirits that I'd pissed off once or twice, although mostly through no fault of my own.

Justina waved at me as Becky sat down on the small bench at the back of the gazebo. My mouth flapped open, but there were too many feelings rocking through my body. My mother and Theresa were clasping hands, staring at Becky as she tuned in. Would the ancestors talk to her?

A few moments of stillness went by. Not one person moved or spoke, each with their gaze riveted on the seer. When she gasped, her eyes flying open, every one of us gasped with her.

A smile spread on her face as tears came to her eyes. "It's true," she said quietly to Gerard. "Devon doesn't need to be disconnected from the ley line if she chooses to be with you. She just has to take her Essex witch vows."

My shaky breath released as my legs gave out from under me. Gerard's arms were around me before I could hit the ground. Tears were like rivulets down my face as Gerard lowered us to our knees, his arms around me, his hands in my hair. A cheer went up around us as we cried together.

Pulling back from where he clasped me tightly, I almost had to tell him to let go. His cheeks were wet, his eyes cloudy from happiness. I bit my bottom lip as I watched him cry happy tears. My man was happier for me than I was. Which shouldn't have been possible.

"I love you," he choked out through the tears. "All of you. No matter what."

Tugging on his shirt, I indicated that he should kiss me, which he did. The others groaned as he swiped his tongue into my mouth and kissed me properly.

When he pulled away, he let go and indicated that I should get up. I did, trying to drag him up with me. Instead, he stayed on his knees.

"Devon," he said.

The whole place went quiet, except for the birds. They sang as the sun started to set and the moon started to show. My hands shook so badly, Gerard had to squeeze them to hold them steady.

"Will you marry me? Now?"

Justina choked back a sob so violently, we all turned to check that she was okay. She waved us on, her cheeks flaming bright red.

"Now?" I whispered, unable to wipe the smile from my face. "Yes. But, how?"

Surging from his place on the floor, Gerard wrapped his arms around me and swung me around. The salt from the circle scattered, making everyone jump out of the way. He kissed me, hard, soft, quickly.

"I can perform a handfasting ceremony," Becky interrupted when he finally put me down.

Looking down at me, Gerard licked his lips as he held my hands. "Shall we?"

"I'll have to think about it, Mr Blow my Fucking Mind."

The smirk that crossed his face made me grin from ear to ear. Glancing around, I sought my mother's gaze. Her eyes were red and swollen, her smile wide. She gave me a thumbs up, reassuring me that I had her support.

"Just get on with it," Kurt said. "All this mush is making me feel nauseous."

"Okay," I breathed, my gaze meeting Gerard's again. "Let's do it."

As Becky got ready, I studied my family. Justina and Kurt had become my best friends. Two people who had seen plenty of shit in life, but let it make them the best agents they could be instead of breaking them down. They'd been the first to ever give me a real chance to do the same. My mother had always loved me, even when she'd been absent. It was my time to support her in our loss.

A brief wave of sadness washed over me just as another white feather floated into the gazebo. My father was here with us, he always would be.

"Okay," Becky started, taking my arm and putting my hand under Gerard's open palm.

A soft blue material was placed over our hands, slowly wound around to join us. As we exchanged our vows, I looked into the eyes of the one man who had gone deeper than anyone ever had. Both of us were ready to leave all the crap behind and start our life together. Was it rash? Abso-fucking-lutely. Did I care? No, not one bit. Life was for living. I was an official Essex witch. I was a normal woman. I was Devon Jinx, and I was finally free

Other Series by Rachel Medhurst

Avoidables

The Deadliners Trilogy

Viking Soul Series

Zodiac Twin Flame Series

Author

Rachel Medhurst grew up in Surrey, England. She writes to prove that no matter where you come from, you can be anything you want to be. Your past may shape you, but it doesn't define you. When Rachel isn't writing, she can be found reading and walking in nature.

Printed in Great Britain
by Amazon